SHADOW JUSTICE

The outlaw trail had been a part of Logan Breck's life ever since the war. He'd made several tries at going straight, but just as he looked like winning, they jailed him — for a crime he didn't commit. The letters from Laurie, his beloved daughter, were his only solace in the penitentiary. Until the day the warden told him of Laurie's death . . . Determined to avenge her, there was only one answer: escape and try to find justice with a six-gun in hand.

CLAYTON NASH

SHADOW JUSTICE

Complete and Unabridged

LINFORD
Leicester

First published in Great Britain in 2006 by
Robert Hale Limited
London

First Linford Edition
published 2007
by arrangement with
Robert Hale Limited
London

British Library CIP Data

Nash, Clayton
    Shadow justice.—Large print ed.—
Linford western library
    1. Outlaws—Fiction 2. Western stories
    3. Large type books
    I. Title
823.9′14 [F]

ISBN 978–1–84617–928–0

Published by
F. A. Thorpe (Publishing)
Anstey, Leicestershire

Set by Words & Graphics Ltd.
Anstey, Leicestershire
Printed and bound in Great Britain by
T. J. International Ltd., Padstow, Cornwall

This book is printed on acid-free paper

For my daughter,
Chris.
Beautiful, loyal, caring, loving.
What more could any father ask for?

1

No Way Out

Once again, there was no letter for him at mail call.

This made three times in a row — three *months* without any word from Laurie.

Something was wrong. *Badly* wrong.

He started as one of the other prisoners, tearing open a package of tattered newspapers he had just collected, said sharply, 'Hell, Logan you're white as a ghost! Bad news?'

Yeah! No news is bad news.

It was there, then, that devastating feeling clawing at him from the inside: the old morale-crushing hunch that reduced him to a sick jelly as one of his greatest fears took hold. But it had to be faced: *Laurie must be dead.*

There could be no other explanation.

If she was merely ill or even injured, she would find some way to let him know. Have a doctor, a nurse, *someone*, get word to him.

Could that sadistic son of a bitch of a warden be deliberately keeping it from him? No, that wouldn't be his way — he gets too much of a kick out of delivering shattering news to any of the convicts under his control.

Back in his cell, Logan made his decision: he was going to find out for himself.

Easier said than done, for no one had ever successfully escaped from Big Mountain Penitentiary. Plenty had tried; no one had been successful: Hadley had seen to that.

★ ★ ★

It was going to take time to arrange, but time was one thing he had plenty of. Sure, he was impatient to be out and away but he was going to do this properly.

First, he had to get back onto the road gang. He had done three months there not long ago for complaining about the slop they called food: if anyone wanted to know the location of Hell, it was a mile outside the western wall of the prison, carving a way over a giant mountain for a stageline that would go broke because of the expanding railroad, even before there was time to use the damn road . . . He would throw a bowl of pigswill in the trusty's face this time. That should get him at least six months on the road gang. But he wouldn't need that long. Despite the killing labour and hardship, the road gang was still the best place if a man was going to attempt escape. Not that anyone had ever succeeded, but taking that first step was easier because the road gang was already outside the high, wire-topped prison walls.

But before he blew up over the grub, there were other things to fix. Like making a deal with the prison barber whose job it was to shave the heads of all convicts, new arrivals as well as inmates. The warden believed that by keeping the hair so short that it was almost non-existent, he had one less thing to worry about: head lice. Body lice he didn't even acknowledge: they added to the inmates' discomfort and Warden Lester Hadley was all for *that!* He allowed beards because fleas and vermin on a man's face could drive him absolutely loco. He called such things his 'little bonuses'.

The man was fanatically determined that his administration of this penitentiary would be exemplary and he worked his staff as hard as he could without inspiring downright mutiny. Hadley had an obsession about saving time, filling out forms well ahead of deadlines, post-dating other official papers, shaving minutes, *seconds*, off daily chores, generally making life hell for both inmates and guards.

Which made it even harder for would-be escapers, because he might change timetables without warning.

Giving up half his tobacco ration, Logan Breck was now eligible for all the dark hair that was normally swept up from the floor of the prison barber shop and dumped. There was a prisoner in 'D' Block who owed Logan a favour: Breck had saved the man's hide once when a couple of hardcase bullies had assaulted him. His name was Piddock, but his prison name was Piggy. A perpetually worried type, he had been something in a travelling theatre before seducing some lawyer's wife behind the scenery and had ended up here in Big Mountain. Best of all, Piggy knew how to make wigs.

There were civilian clothes to arrange, too. The prison uniform was drab grey with big white letters printed on the back of the shirt and down both trouser legs: *Prisoner*. Plus the penitentiary number. Not ideal for travelling in the outside community. Logan had a small stash of money, very small and he used much of this to buy a worn shirt and trousers. Then, after six lashes, he was sentenced to six months on the road gang for hurling his food slop at a trusty. He rolled up his few belongings in an old newspaper, including the stylish wig Piggy had made, hid the package amongst rocks in an area that had already been worked. He could easily snatch this when he was ready to run. Boots were a problem and he hadn't yet solved it. A hat would be good to help hold the wig in place, too. Maybe he'd get one when he was out of the goddamned mountains.

These tangled, mist-shrouded hills with their countless dead-ends and drop-away canyons, clogged with thorn bushes were the reason escape from Big Mountain was so hard. No one knew their way around in there except the Mescalero Apaches Hadley used as trackers. The warden was rumoured to have a secret map too, that, together with the Indians, helped bring would-be escapers quickly to heel. (Hadley was never convinced that some day the Mescaleros mightn't lead him into a trap; maybe cut his throat for whatever was in the store wagon. And so his own map was a precaution). Hadley was a careful man — where his own safety was concerned.

No prisoner had ever managed to find a path through the mountains. Most who attempted it had died trying.

That was the mountains. But the north-facing prison fronted on to a short expanse of prairie with a few old buffalo wallows, it then rapidly deteriorated into a desert, thirty-some miles of waterless, furnace-hot hell, permanently misted with blowing sand and alkali. Beyond it lay civilization, such as it was on the frontier, small two-men-and-a-dog towns, a couple even prosperous because, by a whim of nature, the desert ended abruptly and soon became completely lost in fertile valleys where settlers were now making their homes.

When prisoners were destined for Big Mountain Penitentiary, two heavily armed and equipped cavalry troops from Fort Bigelow escorted the jolting wagons. So everyone from the State Correction Authority down to Hadley himself had good reason to feel smug about the security: the impassable Big Mountain casting its tall shadow over the high walls from the west, while desert sand piled up against those walls from another direction. A position made for a prison that had every right to be dubbed 'escape-proof'.

Logan Breck aimed to change all that.

Breaking out of Big Mountain Pen was only the first step, he realized. Over the mountain was the only way to go — the desert meant almost certain death — only the Mescaleros knew the mountain way.

Piggy, mournful but not dumb, had easily figured out that Logan Breck was planning to take his chances on the run.

'Better if you don't try it,' was his advice.

'No choice, Pig — have to find out what's happened to my daughter. She's only seventeen . . .'

Piggy sucked a hollow tooth and grimaced. 'Such a sweet, tender age!' His porcine eyes flickered over Breck's rangy, muscled form. He was in pretty good shape for a man pushing forty and facing the daily hardships of the prison. One thing about roadwork, it made a man strong, toughened the sinews, even though all the inmates were underfed. 'You're a very tough man, Logan, but this is a big risk.'

Breck merely shrugged, impatient to get away. Piggy placed a soft hand on his forearm, looked up into the grimy, rugged face. 'There's a Mescalero named Birdy — short for 'Bird-Brained' I think. He *is* a mite slow, and sort of off-centre, but he's a friendly soul, loves animals, and can track a bird through a sandstorm.'

Their eyes locked and Piggy smiled thinly. 'I know I'm not much, Logan, but you're the only one who's shown me any friendship, or what passes for it in here — you banged a couple of heads together and saved me from a beating.

It meant little to you, just a casual good deed, quickly forgotten — but not by me.' He looked around at the rest of the prisoners on the brief lunch break and added, softly, 'I make little cotton cords for Birdy to use on his traps and small calico pokes for collecting the nest eggs. As I said, a simple soul — and he'll do anything for me.'

Logan tensed and Piggy added, 'I ask him to, he'll find you a horse and lead you out of here.'

Logan's head snapped up. 'Pig — don't gimme hope where there ain't any!'

'Tell me when you're ready,' Piggy said and shuffled away as one of the scowling guards started ambling across, a brutal man named Collie. They had been talking too long.

'C'mon, c'mon!' Collie growled, holding his carbine menacingly. 'Break's over! Get back to that brush-clearin', pronto! You ain't got ten square feet down to stubble by the time I come back from takin' a leak, I'll bury you

10

there!' He spat and strolled off, scowling.

As Piggy passed close to Logan on his way back to his post, Breck said, 'Tomorrow night.'

Piggy almost broke stride and Breck heard him suck down a sharp breath. 'So soon!'

'Sooner the better.' Logan picked up his short-handled brush hook and headed for the work area, feeling the tension building rapidly in him now he had made his decision.

★　★　★

The best time to go was at the end of the day when everyone was milling about trying to board the open wagons that would take them back to the main prison. It was usually late in the afternoon, but never so late that they wouldn't arrive back at the gates before nightfall.

There was plenty of jostling and shoving, mostly in good nature, for even weary men could find time to hassle the guards in their head-count. The prisoners were hard, self-centred men, killers, rapists, robbers and would take risks to help someone escape, even if they themselves couldn't profit from it. Enemies they may be most of the time, but there was a common bond when it came to standing against authority, which meant Warden Hadley — intensely hated by every prisoner. So these bone-weary men entered into the spirit of disruptive action, even saw it as a chance to settle some old scores, and soon punches were flying and scuffles flared up into real brawls. This evening, at least three became knock-down, drag-out affairs — and the guards were as entertained as the cheering prisoners on the sidelines, shouting encouragement, wanting to see blood flow.

Just to get things started, it had cost Logan almost all of the last of his money plus his old jack-knife with the broken blade that he had managed to hide since he had first been brought to Big Mountain. Laurie had given him that knife years ago when he was mustanging in the Mexican sierras and he was reluctant to part with it. But he had to have a diversion and so he handed it over to Shank Martells who promptly pocketed the knife and drove a fist into the middle of the face of a man standing behind him at the pick-up wagon.

'Your breath stinks!' he growled truculently.

That was all it took. As the hit man swore and staggered, reaching for Martells, another stepped in, jostling, swinging his brush-cutter handle — the guards removed the blades as soon as the day's work was done — and next there was a mêlée with shouting, staggering, cursing men. Breck dropped and crawled under the wagon, saw more bare, muddy feet prancing around on the other side as yet another brawl vied for the guards' attention. He crawled out from under the rear of the wagon after grabbing a battered, leaky canteen that he had bribed the water-carrier to sling above the rear axle. Still crouched, he crab-walked into the brush, dropped to his belly and slithered some yards away from the shouting cursing and howling brawlers.

The noise faded rapidly as he lurched up, doubled over again almost immediately, and made his way into the rocks where he had left his bundle of clothing. With it under his arm, hefting his own brush-cutter handle as a weapon, he sloped away from the wagons and the harassed guards.

By the time they had sorted out the brawl and bleeding, heavy-breathing men were stumbling all over the place, fouling-up the head-count over and over, the guards would only be interested in getting back inside the prison before dark. Warden Hadley would have their balls, sautéd and smothered in onion sauce, for supper if they weren't inside the locked gate by the time the sun disappeared behind the mountain, casting its dark shadow over the compound. By the time they realized the count was one down, it would be too late to get a search under way that night . . .

So far, it had gone according to plan and Logan couldn't believe the rate his heart was hammering against his ribs. He guessed that at the back of his mind, he had felt it would fail like every other attempt to break out from Big Mountain, and now that he was free — for the moment, anyway! — his mind found the fact hard to grasp.

Groping his way into the heavy undergrowth, he stumbled, gasping in shock, as a shadow he had thought was part of a tree trunk detached itself and came towards him. It was Birdy, wearing his shirt outside his britches, belted about with buckskin, a spotted headband holding dull, dry-looking black hair back from his hard-planed face with the high cheekbones and penetrating eyes.

The tensed Breck was crouched,

ready for anything, hickory handle angled for a blow. 'Hell, Bird! I damn near died of fright!'

Broken yellow teeth flashed in the shadow and a gnarled hand gestured for him to follow. He had to be quick! One moment the Indian was there, next Breck was looking around wildly to see where he had gone. But Bird led him to a small draw where there were two horses. One had the wooden Indian saddle with decorated bridle while the other, a roan, Logan thought, had a cavalry-type McClellan saddle and floursack bags hanging from the horn. The reins were rawhide and the single-bit bridle was plaited grassrope. Bird was already mounted and started out of the draw before Breck found the wooden stirrup and swung into the saddle.

It sure felt strange, straddling a horse for the first time in three years! In fact a wave of dizziness passed over Breck as he heeled the animal forward, trying once again to catch up with Bird who was no more than a fast-disappearing shadow now. He had an ear cocked for sounds of pursuit but there was no indication of danger on their backtrail. The Indian said nothing, but once or twice slowed down so that Logan could at least keep him within sight. Darkness closed quickly in the mountains and soon Bird passed back a rope and indicated that Breck should either hold it or tie it to his saddle horn. Feeling like a greenhorn, Breck twisted it about his left wrist, following the tugs and twitches, fighting the skittish roan with his other hand.

Bushes whipped into his face, scraped his arms, jabbed his legs. The horse lurched into and out of holes, causing him to jolt and sway. He had no idea where he was or which way they were headed. Trees were so thick down here that he couldn't even see the afterglow in the sky to get a direction. He knew he could never have made it out of here without the aid of the Mescalero.

'*Muchas gracias*, Pig,' he murmured half aloud. 'This is something I won't forget!'

They came to a stream. He hadn't even heard it trickling over the rocks, the brush was so thick and heavily clustered. The horses drank and Logan stretched out, plunging his hot face under the icy water, gulping a mouthful. Pure nectar!

The Indian was already mounted again and putting his horse across the stream. Logan swung stiffly astride the roan, vastly weary now, and followed. When they climbed steep, lightly timbered slopes, he found Bird sitting his mount silently on a small ledge, looking off into the darkness.

Then he heard it himself. Distant horses, men shouting, no doubt becoming lost very easily in the dark, taking falls, their horses stumbling. Logan stiffened. 'Hell!'

The Indian didn't even look at him, swung his mount away in a different direction to the one they had been travelling. Logan hesitated, then followed: it didn't make any sense to him but he knew he had to place himself entirely in the hands of the Mescalero.

It was not a comfortable feeling, this being 'lost' and disoriented, even though he knew Bird could find the way out. Perhaps he was thinking in a quiet corner of his mind, 'But would he lead me out to safety . . . ?'

He was a villainous looking Apache even if he was supposed to be below average intelligence. But he was a nature man, according to Piggy, and that alone should have put Logan at ease. Should have . . .

They travelled hour after hour and only once more did he hear any sounds that might have meant pursuit. They were a long way off now, though, and he began to relax.

He dozed in the saddle despite his general unease, *Just for a few moments*, he told himself . . . Then — he started when a hand shook him. It was Bird, of course, and the man was holding out a pair of knee-high buckskin moccasin boots. He gestured for Logan to take them and the convict did so, nodding thanks. He thought he must look a mess in his muddy, ragged prison clothes, bare feet, shaven head. It was time to change into range clothes, tug on the buckskin leg boots, try and set Piggy's wig in place.

He froze, suddenly realizing he could see himself, see the muddy clothes, the bare feet, the individual bushes and trees! Daylight! Grey and murky, *early*, but daylight just the same. He looked around. A low range, a distant mesa with a purplish tint in the distance ahead, and, behind him, the massive, bulky towering mountain, bleak, brooding. He couldn't believe he had slept so long in the saddle.

'By God, Bird! We've made it out of the mountains!'

Bird said nothing, pointed across the narrow creek — the last boundary!

— then started to turn his horse, lifting a hand slightly in farewell.

Logan wondered how he could ever repay the Mescalero . . . Then a rifle whiplashed from across the creek. Bird's horse jerked and there was a splash of red as mount and man crashed over into the brush. A second shot knocked Bird to the ground as he struggled to get up, but collapsed.

A third shot slammed into Logan's roan as he rode into the shallows and he kicked boots free of the wooden stirrups and leapt wildly. Before his body splashed into the creek, three men rode across swiftly and levelled their rifles at him as he sprawled in the muddy water. The big guard, Collie, levered a fresh shell into his smoking weapon, eager . . .

'And just where the hell did you think you were going, Breck?' snapped Warden Lester Hadley thickly, as he glanced around. 'By God, you almost made it, you son of a bitch!' Then he grinned wider, triumphantly. 'But

you're wasting your time.' He leaned
forward in his saddle. 'This is all for
nothing — your daughter's dead! Has
been for weeks, you poor fool!'

2

Dead Man Running

Twelve times the plaited rawhide thong cut into the flesh of his back, each time criss-crossing and overlaying the twisted, raised scars already there.

Hadley stood by and watched impassively, flicking a piece of bloody flesh from a sleeve of his jacket once, but otherwise unmoving. Except for his eyes: they glowed and seemed to flicker as each lash curled halfway around Logan's torso and dragged back, deepening and ripping the shallow trench in the pale skin. They were particularly bright if Logan gagged or gasped as breath was beaten from his lungs.

When they cut Logan down — barely conscious now — Hadley watched as the infirmary orderly rubbed salt into the wounds, ostensibly to aid in the prevention of infection, but personally chosen by the warden because of the large sharp-edged coarse rock-salt crystals.

He gestured and Collie, breathing hard from swinging the lash, tossed a pail of dirty water over Breck. He shook his head, lidded eyes half-opening as Hadley stood before him. He grabbed an ear — the hair stubble was much too short — twisted Logan's gaunt, greyish face towards him.

'I believe your daughter's name was Laurie. And only seventeen years old!' He smiled crookedly, moistened his thick lips and made a sucking sound. 'I'll bet she pleasured quite a few men before they were finished with her!'

Logan gave no sign that he understood, or that he had even heard. Hadley sighed, eyes showing his disappointment.

'I don't have all the details but I may be able to find them out — if I do, you can rest assured that I'll pass them on to you with every 'i' dotted and every 't' crossed!'

He chuckled and roughly shoved Logan's head away, drawing a kerchief from a pocket and rubbing his hands briskly with it. 'Solitary,' he snapped to Collie.

'How long, boss?'

''For the warden's pleasure', seems appropriate. I'll make it so in the punishment book — the man's a fool. Things could be so much easier for him if only he would co-operate a little more . . . Ah! Away with him!'

Logan's bare toes scraped and lost some skin as he was trailed across the stone-flagged floor, dragged by Collie.

He didn't feel the jolt when he was flung into the corner of the dark, airless cell in the solitary confinement block below ground level.

Then there was only blackness, shot through with brain-crushing pain and vague moans and shudders.

★   ★   ★

25

Three weeks in solitary, back healing painfully and slowly, the boredom punctuated with beatings led by Collie, the unpalatable 'food' — mouldy bread and stagnant water — tossed carelessly through the small rectangle cut low down in the heavy timber door. There was no light. No windows. The very air was foul, the only freshness coming in beneath the door at times when the wind was right and blew down the stone stairs and along the narrow corridor hewn out of living rock.

Logan took to sleeping with his face against the bottom of the door. There was no bedding so one part of the stone floor was as comfortable as another. He had rub-marks on his shoulders and knees and hips but there was nothing he could do about them. No one spoke to him: the guards and the lackies with them, delivering the food ration, were forbidden to utter even one word. If the prisoner spoke to them — well, it was punishable by yet another beating.

Then, a couple of days past the three weeks, as the flap was lifted and the garbage food tray pushed through, Logan stiffened. A familiar voice spoke before the flap was lowered. 'How you doing, Logan? Back healing OK?'

It was Piggy. And he had barely spoken the last word when there was a roar from the accompanying guard, a scuffle, the sound of blows and something slamming violently against the door, shaking it in its frame.

'You dumb bastard!' *That* voice was easily recognizable: Collie. 'Why in the name of hell did you have to go an' do that?' More sounds of heavy knuckles striking human flesh, more rattling of the door. 'Stupid, stupid, stupid! Christ almighty, you know you ain't allowed to speak to prisoners in solitary! An' you damn well know what it means — unless you got a sudden lapse of memory!'

'I — I was worried about him!'

Logan heard Piggy's whine through the door immediately before Collie's

27

fist began hammering the man's face and body.

'Answerin' back! I just don't b'lieve this! All right, you knothead, you asked for it! Now you got time in solitary an' if there's one peep outta you I'll come into the cell with you — and it won't be to shake your hand!'

And this was how a bloody, semi-conscious Piggy was later thrown into the vacant cell on the other side of Logan's. More dire warnings from Collie and other guards and then the door at the head of the stairs slammed with its usual booming finality.

Logan hurried to the peephole at head level cut into the door. Days earlier, he had broken free a long sliver of hardwood from the edge of the door with his horny fingernails. Now he used this to push through and reach the flap on the front of the peephole, tilt it aside. There was only the almost total darkess and silence of the passage beyond.

'Pig! Pig!' Logan called hoarsely. 'You

hear?' No reply. Logan tried again and again. 'Break a splinter off the door edge and push the peephole flap out so we can talk.'

Sometime during the night hours — he calculated roughly — there was a kind of unintelligible grunt from Piggy's cell. 'OK, Pig! Not too loud. Sound carries easily. If you see a band of light in the passage it means someone's coming through the door at the top of the stairs.'

It was almost daylight by Logan's calculations. Then Piggy's strained voice reached him. 'Logan! I — I'm ready!'

'Good, Pig! What made you speak up like that? Judas, man, this is no place for a holiday!'

He thought the man chuckled and he was surprised after what he had heard when Collie was beating him.

'You're telling me! Logan, have to be quick in case they come. They gave me an orderly's job because I cut my leg badly clearing brush — might even end up losing my foot . . . '

'Jesus!'

'Never mind that — I had to tidy Hadley's office and I looked in the punishment book to get some idea of how long they were going to keep you here.'

'Aw, thanks, Pig, but you shouldn't've risked it! I can take whatever they hand out.'

'No you can't, Logan — Hadley's going to kill you!'

Stunned, all Logan could say was, 'You sure?'

'Your death's already written up in the book. You know how Hadley likes to get ahead with paperwork. I quote: 'Breck, Logan, aged 39 years. A hardened troublemaker, has attempted escape three times. Severe punishment does not deter him. But this time the fool attempted to cross the desert and his body, much the worse for wear from the elements and prowling carnivores, has been found and positively identified. He will be missed by no one.'

Hadley's signed it. And, Logan, the date is Monday — three days away!'

Logan was still tongue-tied as it sank in. Certainly this was as clear a case or premeditated murder as he had ever heard of. *And he was to be the victim!*

'Why, Pig?' he asked eventually. 'Why does Hadley want me dead? I didn't think he'd finished with me yet.'

'I guess because you made it off the mountain — Bird got you off it and out onto a trail that could've taken you almost anywhere. First time it's ever happened and Hadley won't have that kind of blot on his record! If you're dead, dying while trying another escape, that's an end to it. The record stays unchanged: no one ever escapes from Big Mountain, sure not while Lester Hadley warden.'

'Pig, I — I can't even begin to thank you for this. I — don't know what to say. You've taken one helluva risk just to let me know.'

'And you could've gotten killed stepping in to save my hide from those two hardcases that time. No one has ever stood up for me before, Logan. Not even my own brothers. They all thought I was effeminate because I showed an interest in theatre and the stage, costumes, make-up and scripts . . . '

His voice trailed off and Logan shook his head in the darkness. He was still at a loss how to thank Piggy for what he had done — was doing.

'All I can say is *muchas gracias*, Pig. At least I'll be on guard now.'

'You'd better be! It's Collie who'll be taking you out into the desert . . . ' He let that sink in, then added, 'Look at it this way, Logan: *if* you can get away you're home clear. Your death is already officially registered. There will be no search made — you'll be a dead man running and no one'll be after you!'

Logan could see that. All he had to do was escape from a cold-blooded killer like Collie in the middle of a waterless desert without food, water or weapons.

That's all. Then he was home and clear!

*　*　*

They came for him after breakfast. Strictly speaking, they came for him at breakfast time, but he was not given any bread, only a drink of cloudy water. Then he was dragged out of the cell, taken to the bath house and told to climb into the communal bath — a giant molasses keg from some distant brewery filled with sludgy water — and scrub up.

He was given a slightly cleaner prison uniform, no shoes, of course. In fact, Collie was wearing the buckskin half-boots Birdy had given Logan. The guard was about Logan's size, even down to his boots it seemed . . . In Hadley's office Collie stood by with a cocked rifle.

The warden was sitting behind his desk, having just finished a plate of bacon and eggs and toast. He now

33

picked up his coffee cup and sipped, looking at the prisoner.

'You broke my rules, Logan, and now you have to pay for it . . . but tell me, why have you persisted in trying to escape? I can savvy this last time, when you were wondering if your daughter had come to harm,' he smiled. 'And I am, of course, pleased to confirm that she has! But those other times, three altogether. Why did you take such risks?'

Logan bored his steely grey eyes into the smug warden, determined not to let him know he had been prewarned. 'Because I don't belong here!' he answered flatly.

Hadley went very still, frowned slightly, then flicked his gaze to Collie who stood there like some wooden African idol Logan had once seen a picture of, tall, bunched muscles and a blank look that somehow indicated a total lack of care for any human being. The warden suddenly chuckled.

'My God, Collie! Did you hear that?

He doesn't belong here! Oh, for a dollar every time I have heard those words spoken in this office!' He let the chuckle fade and leaned forwward, glaring now at Logan. 'None of us *belong* here, you son of a bitch! But we are here for various reasons. Me, yes, through no fault of my own!' His eyes clouded momentarily. 'Collie, too — because we administer punishment and, let us be generous, sometimes rehabilitation, for you miscreants! You know damn well why you're here! You committed crimes against society and now you must pay. And I am more than pleased to help you settle your debt. Now, does that set you tiny mind at ease, Logan?'

'Not by a damn sight — *I* know why I'm in here, and why you were so glad to see me.' He smiled faintly. 'We haven't had a very satisfying acquaintance, though, have we, Warden? You still don't know what you think I know . . . '

He saw at once that he might've gone just that little bit too far and hastily tried to cover: otherwise he could die right now.

'Maybe I broke the law a few times in the past, but this last time it was just *assumed* I broke it because of my past record.'

Hadley, still looking ugly with seething anger, suddenly spread his arms. 'Well, you can hardly complain! You've robbed banks, stagecoaches, even a train! Why wouldn't a court of law assume your guilt?'

'It happened to be more convenient for them, that's why. They wanted me out of circulation — I wanted to stay free so I could look after Laurie! As it turned out she was a lot more capable of doing that herself than I gave her credit for, but now . . . '

Hadley's eyes narrowed. It was clear that he badly wanted to taunt Logan about Laurie and her fate — whatever the truth of that was — but something in the convict's eyes warned him not to push his luck. He saw Death staring back at him and while it angered him that anyone could look at him in that way and bring him out in a cold sweat in his own office, he held back, perhaps content enough knowing Logan was being sent to his death very soon. 'It would seem that now, you have nothing left to live for, Breck!'

'You might be surprised. If Laurie's dead — '

'Oh, she is I assure you. And if you so much as hint again that I am in any way a liar, I'll — ' He got a hold of himself and sighed, tapping fingers against his empty plate, cutlery rattling. He flung a glare at Collie. 'Just go! Take him to Papago Wells. Let someone else worry about him.'

'Long haul, boss,' Collie said on cue, and Hadley nodded. 'Lots of dangers in that desert.'

'Yes, indeed. But we must be seen to have the future welfare of our — er — charges at heart.' He gave Logan a twisted smile. 'You may be surprised to know that someone believed your story, whatever it was you told the court three years ago, and you are due for a hearing that may even lead to a retrial. Personally, I think it's a waste of time, but I must follow instructions. Now, get him out of my sight, Collie, and take him to meet his . . . destiny!'

He threw one final glare at the puzzled Logan. Was the man serious about a retrial, or was this just a cover-up excuse for taking him out into the desert?

He was about to find out — the hard way.

3

Nothing to Lose

Once in the midst of what, from the prison walls, looked like a dense layer of fog, Logan found that the band of grey-white, endlessly moving haze, was given visual solidity by the intense sunlight.

Its depth was only about eight feet and a mounted man could stand in the stirrups and see over the lower layer. It was like looking at clouds from above — or as Logan imagined it would be. Topography was blotted out, except where, maybe the beseeching arms of ancient Joshua trees reached up through the murk.

Later there would be boulders, heat-cracked, dessicated, shimmering. Somewhere far distant he even saw the blurred outline of a knoll. Then, beyond

— nothing but blinding white sand and alkali. The real desert.

Blinding, because the haze ended abruptly, as if slashed with a knife, and the eye-searing glare stretched ahead to be lost in an even stronger blaze. Collie had his hatbrim tugged low over his eyes and a bandanna pulled up over his nose and mouth, but Logan had nothing: no head covering, no filter for the gritty sand and alkali particles kicked up by the mounts. He coughed and hawked and he knew Collie was smiling behind his bandanna mask, because Logan was losing moisture more swiftly all the time.

What had surprised him was the mount, an old bony mule without a saddle. But he had expected to be dragged, on foot at the end of a rope, behind Collie most of the way. Or as far as they planned to take him before killing him, anyway.

He knew how they were going to do it, too.

Collie had an extra leather gun boot

on his saddle: the scabbard for the Winchester rifle on the right side, but on the left was a stubby, bulging holster that contained a sawn-off shotgun with twin barrels. Normally the guards did not carry these unless there was a danger of riot within the prison. Usually two guards escorted a prisoner anywhere they had to go beyond the walls, too, but this time they obviously wanted no witnesses so there was only Collie. A blast with that sawn-off and Logan would be dead meat — 'shot while attempting to escape . . .'

And with his past record of escape attempts no one would query it.

His hands were manacled but he could use the rope halter to guide the mule who seemed willing enough at first to travel where Collie wanted to go. But once they cleared the haze and the glare hammered at their hides and faces, especially the eyes, the animal began to balk.

Collie had likely expected it but it

didn't make him accept it any more easily.

'Keep that jughead on track, damn you, Logan!'

'I'm no magician. He goes where he wants to.' He held up his manacled hands. 'Unless you'd like to unshackle these so I can control him better?'

Collie snorted at such a request and the look he threw Logan should have taken the man's head off. 'Just keep him followin'!' Then he added half-aloud, 'It won't be for much longer . . .'

Logan pretended not to hear but he figured there was at least twenty miles of desert to cross yet before they reached the valley where Papago Wells nestled.

If Collie had his way, Logan would never see the place. His 'destiny', as Hadley had put it in his records book, was to be a minute patch of searing alkali and gritty sand that would soon cover his remains.

Not if he could help it!

Now that Piggy had forewarned him and he knew what to expect, he had become that most dangerous of all creatures who walked this earth — a man with nothing to lose.

★   ★   ★

Collie didn't waste any water on Logan. The guard had brought three large saddle canteens with him and he drank frequently, if sparingly, watching his prisoner each time but unable to read anything but resignation on Logan's blistering face.

'Man, that's *goooood*!' Collie taunted, but the smile dropped off his face just before he pulled up his bandanna mask again when Logan rasped, 'Enjoy it while you can, Collie.'

The guard frowned, stopped with his mask pulled up halfway. 'The hell does that mean?' Logan shrugged. 'Damnit, I asked you a question!'

Logan turned blurred, raw-looking eyes in his direction. 'Even three canteens won't see you across the Death'shead the way you drink.'

Collie paused, then laughed harshly. 'Maybe they won't have to!' He glared then spat. 'Aaagh! You dunno nothin'. Now shut up and keep that damn mule movin', or you'll end up as dead as Piggy. They oughta be buryin' him by now.'

That froze Logan's belly, though he knew Collie had deliberately thrown it in for its shock value. *Poor old Piggy*. It was not unexpected but — 'One of us might end up dead,' Logan conceded softly, coldly. It earned him two solid backhanders.

Then Collie began caressing the cut-down polished wooden butt of the shotgun, in a good mood now. Logan knew it must be getting close to the place where he was to die. And Collie was looking forward to making his try. *So was Logan: Piggy had risked his neck for him — died to help him.*

The sky was like sheet-iron just pulled from the furnace, heat radiating in solid waves, making men and animals gasp just with the effort of trying to breathe. It crawled relentlessly towards high noon and the pace had slowed appreciably. The sorrel was beginning to show signs of skittishness now. The mule gave a couple of protesting brays but this only earned it a kick behind the ear from Collie, the man riding in close to deliver it. The mule snapped with big teeth.

Logan sagged on the animal's back, slumped, swaying. He almost fell once and Collie swore, edged in and straightened him up. 'You stay put! Won't be long now!'

Those chilling words groped through to Logan's heat-stressed brain and alerted his abused body, setting free the chemicals of survival for self-preservation, a mighty powerful incentive for the human body to start working towards the actions that would ensure survival . . .

He groaned and swayed wildly back and forth, angled out impossibly, almost past the point of balance. The guard rode in fast, reaching for him. 'Goddammit! I said to hold on!'

Logan came back to life.

In a blurred, thrashing movement, his manacled hands grabbed Collie's reaching arm and yanked hard, his heels kicking the flanks of the labouring mule at the same time. The animal bucked, rather than lurching forward, in a surprise movement that suited Logan better.

Because the mule slammed into the sorrel, which instinctively swerved, whickering. Collie came flying out of the saddle as Logan tightened his grip on the man's arm. But he was an old hand at fighting prisoners trying tricks on him. He managed to ram his head against Logan's and they fell to the sand together, rolling. Choking with the alkali rising into his throat, Logan snapped his head forward across the bridge of Collie's nose. It cracked and blood spurted but it hardly slowed the tough guard.

He was in much better physical shape than the half-starved prisoner, but he didn't have the same incentive driving him. He was confident he could overpower Logan and was probably diverting some of his thoughts to how he would savour his revenge once he did so when he should have had all his energies concentrated on this man who had nothing to lose.

He grabbed at Logan's throat and the prisoner tucked his chin down low, foiling the grip briefly. Collie punched him and Logan took it, grunting as the knuckles cracked against his forehead. Skin split above his left eye and then he brought up the manacled hands and, stretching the short chain to its limit, dragged it tautly across the other's eyes.

The guard roared and heaved up, smashing instinctively at the man beneath him. But Logan was already rolling, kicking with calloused feet as hard as any leather boot sole. He connected somewhere, felt Collie's body flinch and stagger. Turning onto his face, drawing up his knees beneath him, Logan thrust with his chained hands, lurched up, spinning back towards Collie.

The guard, hardened by years of brutal work in various prisons, was already recovering and closing in. He groped for his six gun now and Logan scooped up sand with both cupped hands and flung it into his face. Collie yanked his head aside but some hit him and stung his already inflamed eyes. He yelled as the alkali burned, and dragged his gun free. He started shooting wildly, unable to see properly, and the mule snorted and honked, its forelegs folding beneath it. Collie stumbled over the wounded animal and sprawled, smoking gun swinging, searching for Logan. The prisoner was running, staggering towards the sorrel which had backed off with wary, rolling eyes. It started to lunge away but Logan threw himself bodily, hands reaching up, hoping to grab the horn. He could lift his legs and hang on while the horse ran, keeping it between him and Collie . . . he missed.

The horse lunged away and Logan began to fall, hearing the Colt blast again. His groping hands instinctively closed on something. There was a momentary hang-up, and then a jerk as rawhide snapped and he crashed to the sand, rolling again, clutching a bulky object to his chest.

It was the sawn-off shotgun, still in its boot which his weight had torn from its strap on the sorrel's saddle.

Collie had planted his legs solidly. His bloody, gritty face showed brief alarm, and then he lifted the Colt again, thumbing back the hammer.

Logan's fumbling hands found the hammer spurs on the shotgun and he squeezed the triggers instantly. The thundering blast blew the base out of the holster and drowned the sound of the six-gun. Collie's body was flung back a yard before he twisted and fell belly down, blood splashing and rapidly soaking into the desert.

Gasping, blinking, Logan got his legs

under him one at a time, lurched up. The sorrel had run off twenty yards and the mule was gasping its last, still on its knees. He staggered across to Collie, still holding the smoking shotgun in his manacled hands.

He used a bare, horny foot to turn the man onto his back and grimaced.

Death'shead was a good name for this desert. But not for Collie. He no longer had a head at all.

★　★　★

By the time he rode the staggering sorrel into Papago Wells, Logan couldn't recollect how many days it was since he had killed Collie and buried him.

His face was swollen and burned black, despite his bushy beard. Collie's clothes fitted reasonably well but they were soiled from sweat and alkali. The only decent articles he wore were the buckskin halfboots. The six gun in its holster was half-filled with sand. He no longer had the sawn-off shotgun: it was buried with what was left of Collie, the man now dressed in Logan's prison clothes. He had left his few belongings in the pockets: they would help establish the identity of the headless corpse as that of Logan Breck.

What had surprised him most he found in the floursacks that had been hanging on the dead mule: his getaway clothes and other articles he had gathered for his initial escape, including the wig. Seems Collie would have planted these things beside Logan's body: that way it would be easier to assume Logan had intended to attempt escape in the desert all along and had come prepared. But the wig was an asset, and he had used the old shirt he had bought in prison because Collie's had lots of blood on it from the man's violent death. He figured he looked pretty much like a bone-weary prison guard who had just crossed thirty-odd miles of desert. That was a bluff he had to carry off, anyway.

Dismounting stiffly at the hitch rail outside the sheriff's office, Logan knew he was taking a chance. But he had never heard of Collie ever bringing a prisoner all the way to Papago Wells and was almost certain that Sheriff Wilde had never met the dead guard. If he had, well, things were going to get mighty interesting.

Wilde was a bleak-eyed man in his late forties, frontier-weathered, suspicious of his own shadow. He read Collie's identification cards Logan showed him and listened, expressionless, as Logan talked, after he had been given a long drink of water and a short one of whiskey. He kept Collie's hat on, not trusting the wig to stay put on its own.

'Fool made a run for it — I mean, I was bringin' him here with the chance of a retrial that could clear him, but the damn fool *ran*.' He snorted and shook his head. 'On a jughead mule, would you believe?'

'Don't have much choice, do I?

52

You're the only witness to whatever happened so I gotta believe you.'

It was a dry, no-nonsense comment and Logan knotted-up some inside. He decided Collie had been the type to bristle at something like that so he shifted in the chair, glared across the desk. 'Well, you just believe what you damn well please, Wilde! I'm tellin' you what happened and what I'm saying is gospel: Logan Breck made a run for it. He wouldn't stop even when I shot that blamed mule out from under him.'

'Quick with a gun, aren't you?'

'Not quick — fast — when I have to be! I nailed that mule and he somersaulted. Then Breck got up and run at me, reaching for my throat even with his hands manacled.'

'So you shot him.'

Thinking again of how Collie would play it, Logan nodded curtly. 'Blew his damn head right off his shoulders!'

Wilde tensed. 'Judas priest! You have had a high of time of it . . . ' He glanced past Logan's shoulder and out the door. 'Little late to be startin' out tonight.' He tapped a thick file beside his hand. 'These're the papers they sent me on Breck but guess we won't need 'em now. Tomorrow you can take me to where you buried him and we'll identify him officially.' He grimaced at the prospect of digging up a headless man.

Logan stood stiffly: this was the crucial moment. 'Not me, friend. I got some business to do for Warden Hadley down the line at Fort Bigelow. Kinda urgent he says.'

Wilde almost smiled. 'And what he says, goes, huh?'

'He's the boss. I'll tell you where I buried Breck, near as I can recall, if you insist on diggin' him up.' He grimaced. 'Ain't a chore I'd look forward to.'

'Yeah, well, I might just take your word for it. But you'll have to sign a statement before you go anywhere.'

'Sure. Listen, I'm near broke. How about I get cleaned-up, have some grub, come back here and sign the statement, and you can let me have a cell for the night? Save me some cash — I'd like to get away early, anyway.'

'You ain't backward in comin' forward, are you?' Wilde sighed, spread his hands. 'Well, I only got Frizzy Betts locked-up right now so that leaves three cells freed. Help yourself. Lock the street door when you go in the mornin'. I won't be in till after eight.'

'Some folk get it easy! My days start before daybreak.'

The sheriff was studying him closely now. 'You won't see me that early. Had enough of that craziness in the army.'

Logan stifled a yawn. 'Listen, you wanna write out my statement while I go find a bath-house?'

Sheriff Otis Wilde nodded and picked up a pen. 'All right. You leave my cell in a mess and I'll come after you, though, I tell you true, Collie!'

Logan didn't doubt it, and made his way to the door. 'I'm no hog — thanks for co-operating, Sheriff.'

Wilde didn't look up, beginning to write . . .

When Logan returned, looking a little more spruce — he had even wet the tail ends of the wig that showed under his hat to make it look more authentic — Wilde was sitting at his desk looking impatient.

'You look different without the beard.' He pushed a couple of sheets of paper at Logan. 'Read that, correct it where you need to, and sign it — and don't take long. My wife'll be waitin' supper for me.'

'Nice to see a man dedicated to his job,' murmured Logan beginning to read. 'Sorry, but I can't read fast.'

Wilde stood abruptly. 'I got no use for a smart mouth,' he snapped, jamming his hat on his head. 'Sign it an' leave it on my desk — I'll fix it in the mornin'!'

He strode out, slamming the door behind him. Logan smiled, made a couple of corrections, scanned the cramped script, then signed Collie's name to the statement.

He locked the street door, sat down

at the desk, pulled the file Wilde had indicated earlier towards him and opened it. It was headed, simply, *BRECK, Logan*.

He began to read about himself — and his past misdeeds . . .

★   ★   ★

It took a couple of hours and he pulled the drapes over the window, lit the lamp but kept it turned down low. He was supposed to be mighty weary and Wilde would believe him to be in his cell bunk, sleeping. If the sheriff saw a crack of light showing in the front office he would come to investigate and Logan didn't want that.

He sighed as he closed the file.

He sniffed and wiped a hand across his aching eyes. He had felt the prick of tears as he had read the section that told him that Laurie, in between her schooling, had hired a lawyer who had seen enough discrepancies in the story of Logan's imprisonment to start his own investigation.

It wasn't spelled out specifically in the papers they had sent Sheriff Wilde — all he had to know was that Logan had to have an escort while the judicial hearing was taking place. If the presiding judge considered there was enough to warrant a retrial then it would be duly arranged.

'Laurie, Laurie!' he whispered, tapping a finger against her name written on one of the legal papers as if that put him more closely in touch with her. 'Darlin', you must've spent nearly every cent of the legacy your mother left you on this!' He suddenly tightened his lips and slammed a fist down onto the desk. '*Goddamnit*! And I never even got the chance to see you and say thanks — or — goodbye!'

He had forced his mind away from dwelling on Laurie and what had happened to her. The three years he had spent in Big Mountain, he had only looked forward to her monthly letters, her news, chatty style of writing: it had helped him endure that corner of hell. She had said very little, practically nothing, about trying to get him a retrial, but obviously she had been working quietly towards that exact goal. Something must have happened three months ago when her letters had stopped. He had kept telling himself it was all right, just a delay in the mails, perhaps she was too busy with study or exams — everything but facing up to the one fact he had known deep down all along: she was in trouble. He had tried not to think about the worst kind of trouble she could have encountered but finally, it had to be faced.

Laurie was dead ... He had to believe Hadley, although it was still remotely possible the man had said that merely to add to Logan's suffering and uncertainty.

He found it difficult to breathe for a few minutes and then he forced down the rising emotion and slapped the papers with the flat of his hand.

'Well, darlin', you did your best for me and I'll sure do mine for you!'

The first thing he needed to know — yes, *needed to know!* — was how she had died, where and when. Then he would see about following through on whatever new evidence she had unearthed. Whatever it was it had scared someone and they had — He stopped.

He was supposed to be dead. No matter what, there could never be a retrial now, as long as he was listed as being deceased!

He was free and could stay that way if he was careful, but it galled him ragged to think how that lovely seventeen-year-old girl had given up her time and money, likely taking all kinds of risks, to help him gain that freedom and then she had died before she saw any results.

Well, the answer was plain enough: he would have to backtrack over her movements, tread in her footsteps, right up to the time she had died.

A shiver ran through him.

Just how had *she died* . . . ?

He didn't even know that: but he would find out if it took him the rest of his life.

4

Backtrack

It was a long way to Flagstaff from Papago Wells. He quit the town well before sun-up, knocking up the grumpy storekeeper and buying supplies with money he had taken from Collie's pocket: the guard would certainly have no use for it.

The livery man had been already up and about and Logan swung a deal on the sorrel, changing it for a muscly little grulla and ending with an extra six dollars in his pocket.

The grulla was as good as he had thought it would be and got him to the railhead at Crosstrees just in time to catch the weekly train to Flagstaff. The horse was riding in a box car with the mounts belonging to a trio of cowboys on their way to spend some of the trail money they had earned by driving Spanish cattle across from California. They had a card game going on an upended crate between the hard seats and invited him to play but he had declined.

They hadn't been offended and left him alone as he put up his feet on the seat across the aisle from them, tilted the battered hat over his face — careful not to knock the wig awry — and closed his eyes.

With the monotonous rocking of the rail car and the regular *clankety-clank* of the wheels, he started to doze. In that half-world between waking and sleeping, he thought about those past days when he had ridden with the Chance Foran gang.

Mostly they weren't unnecessarily violent, although they didn't hesitate to use dynamite or even nitro to blast open a safe in a bank or railroad depot. And they weren't tardy about trading lead with pursuing posses. But, unlike some of the outlaw gangs rampaging through the West at that time, they rarely left dead men behind. Quite a few wounded, though . . .

At times, a killing was unavoidable. Like when they had hit the bank in Tango Junction, Colorado.

Hell! That was probably where the whole down-slide had begun, come to think of it . . . Yeah. Clawing their way to get to the top, one last job that would ensure their fame — only to find they had gone as far up as they could — and from here on in it was downhill all the way . . .

One whiskey did it. And a beer chaser.

Chance Foran paid for both when they met in the bar of the Shinbone Saloon, in a two-man-and-a-dog town called Delta on the Gunnison River, Colorado.

They'd known each other before, in dubious circumstances, soon after the war ended. Foran a Yankee, Breck a Reb on his way home. Both had been dying of thirst in a skull-strewn desert

64

and by pooling their knowledge they had pulled through. Though Logan had to admit it was really thanks to Foran that he was still alive: the man had carried him a couple of miles in blast-furnace heat to a muddy water-hole that had been their salvation. Logan was packing a Yankee ball just above the left hip at the time and he had taken a fall on it when his horse gave out. Both afoot by then, he had lagged far behind and figured he had seen the last of Chance Foran. He made himself as comfortable as possible, and then Foran had returned and, without a word, slung Logan over his shoulder and staggered through most of the afternoon heat until they had found the pool of damp mud. Squeezing the thick sludge through sweaty bandannas they had slaked their raging thirsts — and survived.

That had been years ago and, for a time, he and Foran had ridden together. Foran had no use for authority, Yankee, Reb or any other kind. They jumped Yankee wagons and Reb mule trains without showing favour for one or the other. Soon they met other men, northerners and southerners, that one or the other had known during the war.

After they had held up a stagecoach successfully and robbed the Yankee carpetbaggers inside, they had tackled a small bank and the Chance Foran gang had become a fully-fledged wild bunch.

They hadn't lasted long, scattering after a job that went wrong and mostly failing to link up again. One of those who had drifted away was Logan Breck. Now they were together again.

'Thought you must've been a rich rancher by now — you was always dreamin' about a place of your own.'

Logan smiled as they sipped their beer at a corner table in the Shinbone. 'Turned out they were only dreams. Worked the trails, did some mustanging, even a little wide-looping. Got a job as bronc-buster on a big spread in Arizona — rancher had a mighty fine-looking daughter.'

Chance Foran, a rangy man about Logan's age, with a reckless face and eyes that were never still, grinned. 'Well, well, well. You was never a ladies' man.'

Logan shrugged. 'She was kinda — forward. She — er — '

He paused and Foran laughed. 'Don't tell me! I can't picture you as an old married man! Or a daddy?'

Breck looked a mite tense now. 'Her old man wouldn't let me marry her. Bronc-buster wasn't good enough for his daughter, no, *sir*! He had me beat up and kicked me out. Few years later, I found out she'd had a daughter. One day ran into the pair of 'em in St Louis. Kid was a beauty, blue-eyed, blonde curls, dimples and a cheeky smile.'

'Pretty, like her old man, huh?' Foran got no response.

'Kid took to me somehow, but Lisa, the mother, soon ended that. Told me she was married to a cattle agent named Carson who didn't care whose kid it was. But he didn't like me being in town so I took another beating.'

Logan paused. 'Funny thing, the kid found me. She must've been only about six but she doctored me as much as she could. I asked her why and she said I was her Daddy Number One, and she liked me better than Number Two, the cattle agent. Made me feel sort of — queer.'

Foran sobered a little and nodded, toyed with his glass, strangely pensive. 'Yeah: kids. They can get to you, eh?'

'Anyway, somehow her letters started following me all over the country and I learned to write good enough to answer a few. Lisa's husband was killed in some sort of fracas and not long after Lisa died from a sickness and the agency was left to Laurie, who was still a minor. Lawyers had to administer the money, till she turned eighteen, and see she had a good education in top boarding-schools and so on. She kept writing to me and we met a few times — last time was just before I took that deputy's job in Tango Junction.'

Foran sobered swiftly. 'Now, I

remember *that*!'

So did Logan . . .

Drifting again, he was riding across the high plains north of the Salt Fork of the Colorado when he heard sporadic gunfire. Hauling rein he listened. Scattered shots, some thudding, some cracking, others like someone hammering. And, beyond those ragged sounds, the whiplashing of a Winchester. Regular, spaced shots. Someone making his bullets count . . . or counting his bullets . . .

Bunch of Indians got a white man pinned down in a buffalo wallow, Logan thought and spurred his mount forward, sliding his rifle out of the scabbard. He was right: topped-out on a small rise, he saw the white man sprawled in a wallow between the legs of his dead horse, seven painted Comanches riding back and forth, using old trade rifles and muzzle loaders. They had flatbows, too, and saved some ammunition by sending in showers of arrows. The white man's dead horse was bristling with the shafts like a hedgehog.

And he was running low on bullets, Logan guessed. The man held his fire until he was pretty certain of a hit, then took his pot shot. There were three downed Indians and Logan thought two at least were dead. The other one might've been playing possum. He might've moved but he wasn't sure.

Logan climbed down, got his mount behind the boulders, then sprawled between two granite outcrops and began shooting. His first four shots brought down two Indians and slammed another far over in the saddle, causing him to drop his weapon. He managed to cling to the horse's mane and was obviously out of the fight. To make sure, Logan brought down the racing horse and it crashed sideways, on top of the wounded brave, crushing him.

The others spun their mounts, soon picked up Logan's position and began shooting, two riding in recklessly with chilling war cries. They both died before they had spurred a dozen yards and the others suddenly stopped shooting, fighting their nervous mounts. Two more shots buzzing past their ears made them decide they had had enough and they spurred away, not looking back.

Logan reloaded, saw the Indian he had suspected was playing possum rear up behind the white man who was standing now, rifle down at his side, shading his eyes as he looked up at Logan. Breck snapped closed the lever on his partly reloaded Winchester, threw the rifle to his shoulder and triggered, all in one swift, smooth movement. The white man dropped instantly, rolling onto his back in time to see the 'wounded' Indian going down with his chest blown open, a hunting knife falling from his grasp. His face seemed white as he turned back towards Logan. He took off his hat and waved.

'Come on down! I sure would like to shake your hand, mister!'

The man was a lawman, which gave Logan something of a start although he was a long way from where wanted dodgers about him might be circulating.

'Tate Ansel,' the man introduced himself. 'Sheriff of Tango Junction.' He was a man in his thirties, hard-muscled and right now sporting two bullet wounds. One was on the tip of his right shoulder and blood trickled down his arm, dripping from his fingers. The other was across his lower ribs, bone showing and a deal of blood. He had a little trouble breathing. 'Nice to meet you, Mister . . . ?'

'Logan. Lucky you found that wallow or they'd've got you.'

'You happenin' along is what saved my hide.' Ansell's mouth was drawn down at the corners and his sweating face was greyish under the grime. 'You wouldn't be headed for the Junction, would you?'

'Was going that way,' Logan admitted slowly. 'Looking for work.'

Tate Ansell wadded a kerchief over the side wound and Logan set about binding it in place with strips torn from the lawman's shirt. Ansell watched him closely. 'Cowman?'

'Mostly mustangs, but I've done my share of trail-driving and cowpunching.'

'Dunno as you'd find a ranch hereabouts that'd take you on this late in the season. They just keep a few men on for winter crew as you likely know.'

Logan sighed. 'Be my luck. Thought if I headed south I might find some spreads still working the range.'

'Nah. Gets cold pretty damn quickly in these parts.' He cocked his head on one side speculatively. 'Northers blow down from the sierras. Town's packed with cowboys who've drawn their pay, spendin' it before movin' on, or figurin' on settin' out the winter, not sure which.' He paused again as if making up his mind. 'I guess I could use a deputy.'

Logan snapped his head up. 'You dunno anything about me.'

'Know you can shoot damn good, ain't afraid to stick your nose in agin the odds to save a stranger's neck — I dunno as I need to know any more.' He set his gaze very steadily on Logan. 'Any more, no matter what. I owe you my life and there's no 'ifs' and 'buts' to be considered. Job's yours if you want it. Ain't too much of a chore and once I get over this wound, we'll tie that town down tight and be able to take it easy by a potbelly stove with soothin' sippin' likker. You could do worse.'

Of course he could — he wasn't loco enough to turn down an offer like that. So he became Deputy Logan and walked the night streets of Tango Junction while Tate Ansell recovered slowly — the bullet had cracked one rib and he had to take it easy in case bone splinters damaged the lung.

For a little while, the town actually belonged to Deputy Logan.

Then, there was a vicious brawl in one of the saloons and Logan had to wade in, first with fists, and finally with a gunbarrel. He took a punch in the mouth — which *hurt!* — and knocked a following swing aside before bending his Colt barrel over the head of the wild-eyed drunken trail hand. As the man sagged, another climbed on his back and he ran backwards, crushing the man between his body and the wall. The man's boozy breath gusted in his ear and he stepped away, let the drunk fall to the floor where he lay, gagging.

'I need a hand to get these two into the cells so they can sleep it off,' the deputy panted, looking around, still holding his pistol. He caught the bearded man's gaze. 'How about you?'

'Pleasure, Deputy,' the man said and tugged his hat brim down a little lower over his hairy face as he shuffled forward.

Dragging the semi-conscious men towards the law office, the man from the saloon said quietly, mildly amused, 'Your eyesight failin' you these days, Logan?'

The deputy frowned, paused on the

stoop and looked at the man who pushed his hat back, revealing his face fully. Logan hadn't looked at the man closely before and now stiffened. 'Chance?'

'As ever was, boyo!'

After a slight hesitation, Logan said, 'Good to see you again.'

Later, over drinks in the front of the law office, the drunks snoring away in the cells, Logan said, 'What brings you to Tango, Chance?'

Foran drained his glass before answering, setting his restless eyes on Logan's face. 'Some — bankin' business.'

Logan tensed. 'Come into some money?'

'Not yet. Hopin' to pick some up, though.'

'Hope you've got all the necessary legal papers.'

Chance Foran laughed shortly, poured himself another shot of Ansell's whiskey. 'Well, I wouldn't swear to that.'

'Then might be best you try some

other bank — in some other town.'

Foran knew he was being warned off but it didn't faze him. 'No, I got my heart set on doin' business with this here bank. Ain't real big but word is they got plenty of cash behind 'em — the ranches out in the valley have banked their money here to kind of show their support for local business. Sounds like a good deal to me — and the boys.'

Logan leaned forward, face sober. 'Listen, Chance, I've been pretty much straight for a spell now and I find I'm sleeping better.'

'But not gettin' any richer!'

'No. Big money don't seem to have the attraction it did once, though . . .' He let it trail off. He wanted to contribute to Laurie's life, pay some of her boarding-school fees, send her some money to buy a fancy frock or hat or something. He flushed at the thought: damnit, he — he wanted to act like a *father*, a real one. She was his daughter, his blood, and she had a right to expect his support even though he knew she would never ask for it, nor, maybe, ever accept it. Their letters to each other were good, something he looked forward to, although he knew his were pretty poor efforts, but somehow he sensed she enjoyed them just the same. She was a fine kid and deserved better than him. But maybe if he could do some little thing, just to show her he *really* cared, that he hadn't run out on her because he wanted to — let her see he was willing to try to make up for all those lost years. Hell, was it even possible . . . ?

He hadn't contributed to her life so far, but now he felt he had the chance — or had to make that chance. His conscience simply wouldn't let him pass it up. Anyway, it was something he *wanted* to do.

'There're five of us left, Logan,' Foran was saying quietly. 'We figure we'll pull close to thirty thousand, maybe a little more. You'd have an equal share . . . '

All those dollar signs swirled in Logan's head and he knew he had not yet come far enough along the straight-and-narrow trail to be able to resist such temptation Thinking of five or six thousand dollars and how he could use it to show Laurie he wanted to be a real father.

'It has to be tomorrow,' Foran said. 'You can figure out why.'

Logan could: the Wells Fargo Special was due to pick up the bank's surplus cash, over and above the allotted amount that was always kept on hand. It would be returned to head office in Denver in an armoured box with four shotgun guards escorting it, two inside, two outriders. Tate Ansell had told him about it and that he would need to be on duty at the bank when the stage arrived, see the right doors were locked or unlocked so there would be a minimum of delay getting the cash on board the stagecoach. The transfer was the most vulnerable time.

'We ain't about to take on that stage

and the guards,' Foran added. 'They got sheet-iron lining the bodywork of the passenger cabin. That's why there's a twelve-hoss team to pull the extra weight . . . and them shotgun guards are trained to kill.'

'Yeah, it'd be stupid to take 'em on,' agreed Logan, flicking his eyes to Foran's expectant face. 'About as stupid as expecting to rob the bank itself before Wells Fargo gets here.'

Foran smiled slowly. 'Thought of that, but we never expected to run into you, Logan. Now that we have and you're totin' a badge, I can't just let it go by! You gotta see that, man, you're the key to us pullin' this off!'

'I'm not, Chance. I admit I'm tempted, but I don't aim to slide back now. Sorry.'

Foran was silent, took out two cheroots and passed one to Logan. They fired up and Foran tapped his fingers on Ansell's scarred desktop, said quietly, 'We were lucky we never poisoned ourselves at that mudhole in the desert — guess we were meant to survive and help each other out . . . '

Logan knew what the man was saying and wished he didn't. But the fact was inescapable: he owed his life to Chance Foran, had never had any way of repaying him. Until now. So — *there wasn't much choice, was there?*

It all went wrong — not because of anything Logan did, nor even Foran and his men, but because an over-wrought bank clerk took the chance of reaching for the six gun slung on a nail just below the countertop in his cage.

Foran and Whip Dexter were collecting money from two other clerks and maybe the young greenhorn figured their attention was diverted. For he grabbed his Colt and even as he thumbed back the hammer, shouted, almost screaming the words: 'Get your hands up, you lousy thieving snakes!'

He was dead before he finished speaking those few words. Both Dexter and Foran whirled and nailed him with two shots apiece. The clerk shuddered, crashed into the cage and toppled to the floor, gun spilling from his grip. One of the lady customers being watched by two more of Foran's gang screamed and fainted. A townsman made a dive to get out of the street door and was brought down by a single shot, his arm smashing through the etched glass panel in one of the doors.

Someone in the street began yelling and Foran knew it was all over. He didn't waste time on cursing, called to Dexter, and, taking what money they already had, they made a run down the passage towards the rear door.

The door that it was Logan's duty to check and make sure remained locked under all circumstances during the cash transfer . . . Foran hadn't been quite sure of Logan but was mighty relieved when he yanked the door and it opened and he and Dexter spilled out. They began to run to where Phil Daggett was waiting with the getaway mounts.

Behind, men had burst into the bank — after all, it was their savings the outlaws were stealing — and there was a shoot-out right there in the bank's foyer, bullets whistling, smashing glass, punching holes in the plaster walls, splintering woodwork. A townsman was hit squarely and he lurched back, crashed through one of the big street-front windows. The bandit who had shot him was startled and stood up unthinkingly for a better view of his handiwork. A shotgun thundered and the man was blown halfway across the room, his bleeding body falling over the lower legs of a prone female customer. Immediately, she started screaming hysterically.

The other outlaw ran for the shattered window, his gun firing and raking the men crowding in. He leapt over the body hanging half in and half out of the window frame, stumbled, and was brought down by a volley from the street.

Sheriff Tate Ansell, shirtless, his side bandaged, was just reloading his shotgun, looked around and saw Logan, rifle in hand. He gestured wildly to an alley mouth.

'The rear! The rear!' the sheriff yelled, grimacing as he grabbed at his side which was bleeding again, from his exertions.

Logan ran down the alley, making it look like he was going flat out — but he didn't want to get there before Foran and Dexter and Daggett had ridden off. He faked a stumble, heard Ansell yell again, and then righted himself and ran on.

The three outlaws were already clearing the edge of town as he threw his rifle up and fired four fast shots, *one-two-three-four* — spacing out and levering deliberately.

Then a breathless voice said behind him, coldly, 'I've seen you shoot a damn sight better'n that! A *damn* sight better, mister! An' I'll be mighty interested to hear what's suddenly turned you into a goddamned amateur who couldn't hit the side of a house if he was leanin' on it!'

5

Bounty Hunter

Chance Foran's face was set into hard lines as he toyed with his glass in the saloon and watched Logan.

'You shot well enough, damn you!' he growled, his tone taking Logan by surprise. 'You got me under the left shoulder — arm gets stiff in the cold, even when it rains — I get a reminder of Tango Goddamn Junction every time I cough, or breathe deep, like a knife twistin' in my back!'

'I wasn't aiming to hit.'

'An' you shouldn't've been! But if you ever wonder why you never got a share of what loot we grabbed, that's it!' Then Foran shrugged and got up and went to the bar and brought back more drinks. As he sat down, his tone lightening now, he said, 'Well, it was a long time ago — I thought for a while maybe you'd been *tryin'* to knock me outta the saddle, so you could square with Ansell or somethin'.'

'You ought to know better. I said I'd help — against my better judgement, but I needed some cash in a hurry. Anyway, Ansell fired me for not stopping you getting away.'

'That all?'

'He could've locked me up. But I'd saved his neck, so he gave me that much of a break. Said if I ever poked my nose over his County Line again he'd nail me, either kill me or lock me away till I was tripping over my long grey beard. That's as square as Tate Ansell and me'll ever be.'

Foran arched his heavy eyebrows. 'Sounds like he was kinda upset.'

Logan nodded, pensive. 'You could say that. He also went easy by not checking out the wanted dodgers — suspected there might be one out on me — but I'd saved him from those Indians . . . Way he saw it I let him down at the bank fracas — and he was right.'

'Hell! You developed a conscience?'

Logan lifted his gaze slowly. 'Mebbe — I want to stay out of trouble, Chance. I want — I want to do right by Laurie. I don't want her to feel ashamed of me.'

Foran blew out his cheeks. 'Well — And here I was thinkin' you're just the feller I need.' He smiled as Logan tensed. 'Got this big deal that'll set us all up for life.'

'Life imprisonment, most likely. I'm kinda familiar with your 'big deals', Chance. They never seem to work.'

'Don't go soft on me, Logan! Chris'sake, man! You want money to get you in good with your kid? OK, I'm givin' you the chance. My folks didn't *name* me 'Chance', you know. They called me Asa — I earned the nickname because when I seen a chance to make some fast money or saw a way out of a tricky deal, I took it, ran the risk. And it worked. I ain't never been in the pen.

Couple days in some hick lawman's cellblock behind his office, is all. We could come outta this one with a real stake, Logan. It's like Fate brought us together here tonight.'

'Well, Fate tripped up and fell on its face.' Logan stood. 'I'm gonna try to make good, Chance. Anyone gets in my way and . . . '

Foran looked slightly alarmed, holding up a hand.

'Whoa! No need to threaten me — I don't take to threats, you oughta know that — an' remember it.' He sighed heavily. 'Dunno how we got to this point but — I could really use you, Logan. I know we could pull it off if you'd join us. I'll tell you: it's a train and it's dangerous, I'll be square with you on that, but it's worth it, man. You could come out with — aw — twenty, thirty thousand.'

That did it for Logan.

When Chance Foran started throwing around figures like that, there was bound to be a lot of fantasy in there somewhere. Halve it and then halve it again and you might get somewhere close, but it would still be an exaggeration.

Twenty, thirty thousand! The man must really think he was a damn fool to believe that.

Be nice, though . . .

He held out his hand and Foran took it slowly. 'Good seeing you again, Chance. Now we've come to the parting of the ways. *Adios*.'

He hoped that sounded as final as he meant it to be.

Foran seemed reluctant to let go of his hand now, stared levelly into Logan's face. 'You're makin' a mistake, *amigo*. Gospel. This could really set you up. You could impress your kid seven ways to Sunday and then some.'

'Not if I'm in jail or dead, Chance. You know I'm stubborn. If I say 'no', I mean it.'

Foran let go his hand as if it was suddenly crawling with maggots. His face was stiff. 'Yeah, OK.'

That was all. No 'so long', or 'good luck'. He just turned on his heel and walked out of the Shinbone saloon . . .

★　★　★

Logan Breck made his try at riding the straight and narrow trail and he did pretty good for a while. Busting broncs here, capturing mustangs in the high country just before winter when the snow drove them down into his waiting traps, riding drag on a couple of trail herds and, man! that was real dedication! He must have swallowed half the southern States in the choking dust clouds of those herds. He trapped for a while but though the money was good, a man had to wait too long to get his hands on it, build up a big pile of pelts before he could go claim it. And, if the market was all askew, he mightn't even make expenses.

In all that time, he hadn't heard of any great train robbery that might be associated with Foran. In fact, he had not heard a solitary thing about the Chance Foran Wild Bunch since Foran walked out of the Shinbone saloon that day . . .

He slowly built up a small nest-egg and deposited it in the Dogwood branch of the First Federal bank while he looked around Raintree Valley for a quarter section he could build up into a small spread. He was busting his butt, determined to make Laurie proud of him.

The letters were still coming from Laurie and they had met twice. He was nervous and belly-knotted each time but she was at ease, casual and loving, and he felt a warmth in his hard body he had never known before. Maybe he was subconsciously trying to give out some of the parental love he'd never known himself . . .

'Given any thought to what you might do when you finish your schooling?' he asked her as they were having supper in a hotel in Carraway Creek. It would be their last meal together this time for she had to leave for Denver and return to the Boarding School on the morning train.

He loved that serious look she got on her young, oval face with the candid blue eyes and the soft mouth that would make some lucky ranny mighty happy one day. 'Yes, Dad — ' He loved that part too: *dad*. 'I'm good at figures and I have quite a bit of Mother's legacy left, so, seeing as you won't let me help you — ' She paused waited for him to say something but all he did was wink at her. Smiling faintly, she continued: 'I — I thought I might open an accountancy.'

He blinked. 'What's that?'

She smiled again, gave a small, warm-throated laugh as she closed one small hand over his calloused knuckles.

'I mean to employ several good accountants and hire them out to ranches or firms who might not run to paying a full-time one — I know it will take some time to set up and for me to earn a good reputation because I'm so young. I'll only be eighteen when I finish school — but I can afford to carry on for a year or so, working up a business, if I'm careful. I'll buy expert advice until I know as much as the experts I hire.'

'Well, can't fault that, Laurie! Dunno where you get the brains from. Sure not me, and Lisa — well, I guess she was her Old Man's daughter and he was pretty sharp with a dollar — as well as his tongue and hired muscle. Never split a knuckle himself. He could afford to pay to have it done.

Laurie laughed again. 'I love the way you talk, Dad! I'll also be in a position, I hope, dealing with cattle agencies and range associations' accounts, perhaps to help you in your ranching . . . '

He had to smile, didn't aim to knock the edge off the kid's enthusiasm by a flat refusal. 'You just never know, might be nice to have someone to turn to in my old age.'

'Oh, you'll be successful long before

then! I'll see to that!' She finished with a cheeky smile.

Yeah — there was everything to admire in young Laurie: she might be reaching high, but she knew it wasn't going to be easy and was ready for the long haul. In a girl only in her teens, it was nothing less than — wonderful. Of course, Logan was strongly biased, he admitted that — to himself anyway, and . . .

Those days were good, really good. A whole new experience for him, gave him the best memories . . .

Then the unthinkable had happened: the First Federal Bank at Dogwood was robbed of every cent within the big iron vault that had been specially built-in to deter thieves. He, along with many others, lost all of his savings and for some reason the Bank's insurance had been allowed to lapse, so there would be no recompense available.

He was ruined and had no choice but to go back to drifting.

Of course, he never told Laurie. He

wrote upbeat letters as well as he could, made them short, pleading lack of time because he was so busy either building up his small spread — which had now gone to creditors — or on a contract job with some cattlemen's association.

He never knew whether she was fooled by it or not: he had a notion that she could read between the lines. But if she *had* suspected he was broke she wouldn't insult him by offering money from a distance. She might turn up unexpectedly sometime and offer him cash, but it would be face-to-face — he kind of hoped she would appear. The cash didn't matter a hill of beans, but seeing her again would be mighty fine . . .

Then the news broke.

It had been the Chance Foran gang who had blasted their way into the First Federal's vault, using a notorious explosives expert named 'Nitro' Galloway.

Galloway had grown careless on another job and a massive blast had hurled him through a splintering clapboard wall, causing him terrible injuries that eventually proved fatal. The same blast also killed two other members of the gang he was working with at the time. On his death bed, Galloway had confessed to several crimes — including the First Federal Bank robbery in Dogwood, with Chance Foran.

It was just as well he died because he would not have lived for long, in or out of jail, not after naming so many outlaws . . . especially Foran.

So Chance had finally found the big one after all, Logan thought. The robbery that would set him up for life — not necessarily the surviving members of his gang, too, but certainly Foran himself would live the grand life. And a small portion of that money belonged to Logan Breck.

Foolishly or not, once again near broke with ragged clothes and a jaded horse, drifting the outer edge of trails where jobs were few and far between and winter once again coming on, Breck decided he was going after Chance Foran.

There was a big reward for the man and his gang — five thousand dollars on Foran alone, for several people had died in the robbery, including the son and daughter-in-law of a State senator. Bounty hunters came riding in from all over the country with guns oiled and knives honed.

And Logan Breck became one of them.

But he had a big advantage over the professional manhunters — he knew most of the gang's hideouts. They might not use them now, but it was obvious that the first thing he had to do was check them out.

★ ★ ★

Phil Daggett was at the fourth place he checked, far back in the Hole-in-the-Wall country of Wyoming, way north of where Logan had expected Chance

Foran to run. But the man had half the country hunting him by now and must be desperate — or laying a mighty good false trail. Logan had no choice but to follow until he could prove otherwise.

The original gang had operated from here for two years before Foran decided to move into the big time and try his hand in the faster developing territories and states to the south. But once in a while, Foran had returned because it was a good place and easily defended.

Logan rode in through the narrow, zigzag cutting, rifle butt on his thigh, watching for any fresh tracks. In two places he discovered some: loose earth dislodged by the side of a hoof as the mounts crowded through the knife-blade gap in the towering sandstone walls. Look up and the moving clouds gave the impression of those same walls tumbling inwards: he had seen three posses turn tail and quit without going any further. Claustrophobia was something that not even a law badge could fight.

Logan didn't like the crushed-in feeling, and avoided looking up in case the phenomenon of the tumbling walls flipped his mind enough to make him back off.

He had just left the zigzag when the rifle shot crashed and echoed around the expanding walls of the tear-drop-shaped canyon he had ridden into. The bullet zipped and tore lines of dust from the soft pinkish sandstone, growling away in ricochet.

He spurred his grey into the deep shadow, quit saddle before the horse had skidded to a halt and hit the ground running. He dropped, rolled over and over behind a low line of boulders as three more bullets erupted around him. Panting, levering in a shell as he twisted, he dropped the rifle barrel between two rocks, spotted the slowly drifting gunsmoke and got off his first shot before two more slugs raked his shelter. He squirmed in tighter against the rocks, eyes darting about, selecting a better position. Without taking very good aim, he fired three times as fast as he could work the lever and trigger and while the ambusher was ducking low, he gathered himself and launched bodily to the right, grunting as he banged one leg on the curve of a basalt rock. It threw his line off and he rolled down a small slope.

By the time he had come to a stop, Daggett, impatient as usual, was standing in his rock shelter, rifle at the ready, searching for sign of Logan. He spotted Breck at about the same moment as the man fired upwards.

Phil Daggett was starting to turn and drop back out of sight when the bullet hit him high up in the body. He jerked and floundered, dropped his rifle over the edge and it skidded and slid down to the same level where Logan crouched. He knew he had hit Daggett solidly, dodged between some boulders, crouched for a few moments behind a dusty bush, then charged the slope at full run.

He zigged and zagged, jumped rocks,

rolled across small open spaces, kept moving without pause, rising to his knees, then thrusting up and continuing. Breathing heavily now, he came in around the line of rocks that had sheltered Daggett. And there was the man lying half on his face, blood high up near the collar of his shirt, moaning. Logan sidled crabwise, slightly above Phil, and then eased down. His boots skidded on loose stones and Daggett spun onto his back, firing a six gun across his body.

The lead burned air past Logan's head. He ducked instinctively, slid down further and fired the rifle onehanded. The barrel jumped high but the bullet took Daggett somewhere below the belt and he howled, dropping his Colt to grab at the wound.

'You . . . done for me! Damn . . . you!'

When Logan knelt beside him, the hot rifle barrel pressed into the man's body, he saw that Phil had an older more serious wound on the left side of his chest. The shirt was caked in dark, dried blood and the raw edges of a shotgun wound showed, purple and red with inflammation, oozing poison.

'They leave you for dead, Phil?'

Daggett's face was greyish yellow, gaunted with pain, and now showing surprise. 'Logan! Hell — din' — din' know it was you! Just figured you — for another — bounty hunter . . . '

'I am, Phil.' Logan sat back from examining the man's wounds, thumbed back his hat. 'Sorry, *amigo*, but it looks pretty bad . . . '

Daggett coughed up some blood, spat, and nodded as he grimaced. 'Caught some buckshot in an ambush they laid for us — must be about a — a week ago. You know the old rule . . . '

Logan knew: *no prisoners, hostages or wounded will be allowed to slow down the gang's escape . . . .*Foran's decree.

'Didn't think Chance would make that apply to you, Phil.'

102

'Me . . . neither. But . . . I'm one less to . . . share with. He's got the bunch down to just him and Dexter and Durango Brown now: we picked him up 'cause he has kinfolk all the way up here. Seen Chance push Garvin off a — a mountain trail. Claimed Kennett 'drowned' in a flooded river, south of the Big Salty Rapids. Just him an' Whip an' Durango now — with all that — dinero.'

'Some of it's mine, Phil.'

Daggett's eyebrows jumped. 'Y — your's . . . ? How you fit in . . . ?'

'All the money I had in the world was in that bank vault.'

Daggett, fading fast now, stared a long time, his head moving slowly side to side. 'Well, smoke . . . me! If it didn't hurt so much, I — I'd laugh!'

'I'm going for the bounty, Phil — I need the money and I guess I owe Chance something. You do, too, the way he left you . . . '

Daggett was silent, his glazing eyes holding to Logan's hard face. Then he nodded, sighing, fighting to get out his last words.

'The Santee Tanks. Gonna grab a train there to Laramie or Cheyenne . . . '

He gave Daggett some water although it wasn't supposed to be good for a stomach wound. But Phil Daggett was too far gone to worry about anything like that.

He died ten minutes later and Logan buried him, found a little food in the man's grubsack he could use and a half-box of cartridges that would fit his rifle.

Then he started on the long ride to the railroad watering tanks at the lonely stop-over called Santee Station.

He had a lot of time to make up.

6

To Big Mountain

The tanks were glaring in the sun, the conical sheet-iron caps almost blinding to a rider coming in from the north-east.

Logan had ridden hard, taking most meals in the saddle, his jaws aching from chewing jerky or hardtack. Phil Daggett had told him that Foran and his men had plenty of time to get to the watering station, but he wasn't sure when the train was due to arrive.

Logan knew the Santee Tanks and the country surrounding them well enough to figure where Chance Foran would camp if he had to wait for the train. Breck's main worry was that the train might have already been, watered, and moved on. Quite a few folk picked up the train here bound for Fort

Laramie: drifting cowhands in from the outer ranches looking for a free or cheap ride, the odd settler needing to get to the bigger towns for one reason or another, farmers with produce to sell. It served a large, remote area.

From Laramie, it was only a frog's leap on to Cheyenne and if he knew Foran, the man would make that part of the journey by horseback rather than stay on the train.

Lawmen tended to hang around the bigger depots, like Cheyenne, on the look-out for men on the dodge. Wyoming Territory at the time, with its wide-open spaces and scattered lawmen and a no-questions-asked policy amongst the far-flung cattlemen, was a popular place with outlaws.

When he reached a knoll with some conifers forming a potato-shaped patch of shadow, Logan reined down and shaded his eyes against the glaring tank tops.

There was no one around — and the big canvas hoses were back on their hooks. But there was a glistening pool of water beneath which meant they had been used not long ago.

Then he heard the distant though still piercing whistle of a train and he stood in the stirrups, moving the horse out of the clump of trees — and there it was! Crawling across brown-grass country under a long banner of black smoke, which was dispersing at its extremity, in ragged black smears across the blue of the sky, but thick and belching at its source — which was the smokestack of the rattling locomotive.

Going away from him!

'Goddamn! Just too late!'

His horse was weary, *he* was weary, in no shape for a long and probably fruitless chase, but — *Wait!* This was flat country here: all the railroads in Montana and Wyoming stayed clear of the hills as much as possible because of the Indian threat. Now he could see three buffalo wallows between him and the gleaming silver horseshoe that could only be the long, wide curve of the railroad tracks.

But he didn't have to follow the miles of curving tracks: he could cut across country in a straight line, ignoring the curve, and pick up the train in less than half the distance as the arc swung back this way, a few miles from here.

It would still be hard on the horse but it was his best chance. And he didn't aim to give up after getting this close ... He kicked the spurs against the sorrel's wet flanks, urging it on with a wild cry.

The horse was staggering by the time he closed in on the rear of the caboose, swaying as the train began to gather speed on a down-slope Logan hadn't noticed. There was a wisp of smoke coming from the small chimney which told him the guard was inside brewing some coffee or cooking grub.

He raked with the spurs reluctantly but had to force the last burst of energy out of the flagging mount. It responded well enough and almost crashed into the rear of the caboose. He made several tries at reaching for the ladder that ran down the end, leading to the roof. He missed, and lashed the sweating, straining horse with the rein ends. He couldn't believe the effort the big mountain sorrel put into that last burst. It took him halfway along the caboose where there was another ladder and he grabbed the sun-hot iron and as the weary horse dropped back, the forward motion of the train literally yanked him out of the saddle. His legs and knees banged hard against the caboose and then his scrabbling boots found a rung, slipped, found it again. He clung there with the wind whipping past his face, hat hanging down his back, hoping the horse would find a good new owner eventually.

The sorrel swerved away, staggering, into the trackside brush. As he swung onto the small platform between the caboose and the rocking cars and freight wagons, he wished he had been able to bring his rifle with him. Panting, rubbing his burning palms, he straightened — and looked into twin gun muzzles.

'The hell you think you're doin'?' demanded the train guard, covering Logan with a Greener shotgun.

Logan made signs of peace, fighting for breath. 'Sorry, had . . . had to get on this . . . way.'

'You did not!'

Logan nodded emphatically. 'Yeah, I did.' He gestured behind him to the closed door of the first passenger car. 'Feller in there owes me a lot of money. Been chasin' him for weeks. Missed him at the tanks — rode across country . . .'

The guard spat, chewed one end of his long, nicotine-stained moustache. 'Yeah, watched you comin' — good hoss, that sorrel.'

'Uh-huh. Sorry to leave it go, but OK if I go through and find this feller I'm after?'

The guard looked at the holstered six gun in its tied-down holster. 'I dunno. I don't want no gunfights on my train.'

'No gunplay . . . ' Logan said slowly.

'No! Can't risk it. You better step in here and we'll talk about it some more . . . '

Logan didn't want that: if the guard had seen him coming, then Foran or the others might have, too. But he nodded and stepped forward as the guard moved aside. Logan spun, knocking the shotgun down and jumped as one barrel exploded into the tarred floor of the platform. *That did it!* Foran would have been alerted by the shot, so Logan clipped the guard on the jaw, caught the man as he fell forward. He eased him back into the caboose, scooped up the shotgun and jumped over to the platform of the passenger car just as the door opened and Durango Brown appeared, gun in hand.

Logan knew him from way back: he had ridden with the gang in the early days, a wild ex-soldier who still wanted the excitement of gunfire and swift action, especially if he could make some easy money at the same time.

And he was trigger-quick, which was one reason they had dropped him at the time. But now Foran seemed to like a bit of shooting with the jobs he pulled. His killer-streak was showing through more and more. A medium-size man, Brown crouched now, blinking, wary of the shotgun.

'Chance thought it was you ridin' in but Whip an' me didn't b'lieve him. No one expected you.'

'Get back in there, Durango!' Logan lifted the Greener, thumb on the hammer. 'It's Chance I want.'

Durango was no hero and hastily holstered his Colt, lifting hands out from his sides. 'Take it easy!'

He turned and stepped back into the car. A woman passenger halfway down the rows of seats screamed when she saw the shotgun in Logan's hands. Behind her and across the aisle, Logan spotted Foran. He didn't see Dexter until Whip rose from behind a seatback and snapped a shot at him. Other passengers started yelling, diving for cover. Durango Brown staggered as Dexter's bullet clipped his shoulder.

'Watch it, damn you, Dex!' cried Brown, grasping his bleeding shoulder. Then he threw himself against Logan, crushing him into the open door. 'Get him, Chance!' he yelled and dropped to his knees, reaching for Logan's legs.

Dexter fired as Foran triggered and splinters flew from the doorway and glass shattered. Logan blasted with the shotgun and the seat back that sheltered Dexter was blown apart, the man hurled back violently against the wall. Foran snapped another shot at Logan and crashed through the doorway at the other end of the car. Logan clipped Durango with the shotgun, flung it aside and went after Foran, palming up his six gun.

'You've got my money, Chance! And I'm coming to get it!' Logan shouted as he ran down the narrow passage between the seats. Passengers cringed and he glimpsed Whip Dexter's bloody form huddled between the seats just before he dived out onto the swaying platform.

The door leading into the other car was swinging and banging with the motion of the train and Logan dived for it. Then a shot blasted from above him and he felt the wind of a slug past his face. He fell back into the first car: Foran, ever the fast thinker, had opened the door leading into the next car forward but had scrambled up the ladder going to the roof instead of entering the other car.

He fired again, lying prone, reaching over the roof edge to shoot at Logan. Breck pushed back as the lead tore up the floor, snapped two fast shots upwards. Splinters exploded in a thrumming fan and tarpaper shredded as Foran wrenched back out of sight. Still crouched, Logan heard the thud of the man's boots running along the roof walkway. He thrust up and started up the ladder, crouching on the rungs as his head drew level with the roof. He eased up cautiously, glimpsed Chance

Foran at the far end. The man turned and stumbled with the jerking motion as the train rounded a bend. His shot went wide and Logan threw himself forwards, one hand clawing for a hold, shooting with the other. Foran was on the next car, now, running, stumbling, putting down a hand to steady himself occasionally. Logan went after him, staggering dangerously, too, saw there was an open-bed freight car in front of Foran, a black tarp covering a stack of boxes, humped up by their shapes. Logan fired, but missed. Foran sprawled on the canvas, rolled off the hump, protected by its bulk.

Logan staggered the rest of the way, prepared to make the same leap. Then Foran rose from behind the tarp, steadied his Colt and triggered. The wind ripped the gunsmoke away and he saw Logan stagger, briefly fight for footing, then topple off the car roof onto the tarp, landing heavily.

Logan was hit in the side, clawing at the canvas to keep from falling. Foran clambered up, and stood carefully balanced, and looked down into Logan's pain-contorted face. Then he kicked him, coldly stomped on his grasping hands, until Logan tumbled off the racketting, bucking train.

He landed in the brush, felt it give way under his weight, the branches cracking one by one. There was a solid jar that smashed the breath from him and the lights dancing behind his eyes went out abruptly . . .

* * *

He was still out of it when the law, summoned from Fort Laramie, accompanied by a small troop of soldiers, found him sprawled in the brush, battered, bleeding, but alive.

There wasn't much to it after that. The next few weeks were pretty hard and everything seemed to be against him: he was the aggressor, had endangered citizen's lives.

Sheriff Tate Ansell was called in from

Tango Junction and he admitted he suspected Logan had been implicated in the bank robbery that had gone wrong. Since that time, he had found a wanted dodger with a description that could fit Logan — a man wanted for robbery and cattle rustling, thought to be one of a lawless gang rioting across the countryside.

There were other things that pointed to him being lawless, but he had clinched his guilt by his own words on the train coming from the Santee Tanks. He had told the old guard he had assaulted that there was a man on the train who 'owed him a lot of money' and he had been trailing him for weeks to catch up with him.

'Sounded like he aimed to kill him when he finally found him,' the guard added, head conspicuously bandaged.

Logan had yelled almost the same words when chasing Foran up onto the roof of the passenger cars. Dexter was identified as one of the robbers wanted for the big bank robbery in Dogwood but Durango Brown had managed to jump off the train and get away. He was still on the loose. They thought Logan had been double-crossed and was chasing Foran for his share of the stolen bank money. And they wanted to know where it was now and, because he couldn't tell them, *wouldn't*, they reckoned, he was beaten and kicked again. Without result.

'The money I wanted was what I'd had on deposit in the damn bank! Foran stole it and I need it — that's all I wanted. That, or to collect the bounty . . . '

Naturally, no one believed him. And to make it worse, he could not prove he had not taken part in the Dogwood robbery: simply because he had been alone in the hills, trying to trap mustangs at the time. No one had seen him, except an old, lone Indian, so he had no alibi.

With his past history and association with known outlaws and killers, his conviction was merely a matter of form.

Innocent he may have been of the Dogwood robbery, but the prosecution twisted it around so that the judge, taking into account his past reckless-ness, sentenced him to ten years in Big Mountain Penitentiary, with no time off or chance of parole. *Ten long, brutal years, hard-time.*

He had done more than three years and had taken much punishment and many beatings. He hadn't understood at first why he had been singled out by Hadley and Collie until one day, after he was hanging by his arms, head down and dripping blood while Collie caught his breath, Hadley said,

'You're a damn fool, Breck! All you have to do is tell us where the bank money is — or where we can find Foran. Then your existence here will improve considerably . . . '

They were after the loot from the Dogwood job and it looked like they wouldn't let up on him until they got some kind of answer they would accept.

That was when he made his first

attempt to escape, realized now how that probably only strengthened their certainty that he knew where the money or Foran was . . . and was going after one or both.

He could not have survived that time except for Laurie's letters. They had sustained him — until they had stopped and he knew there could be only one explanation for that — terrible though it was to contemplate . . .

But if she was indeed dead, she had apparently set in motion an investigation that could lead to a retrial. And Hadley got his orders to escort Logan to the Papago Wells hearing before a judge and other legal representatives. The warden had been afraid someone might believe Logan when he claimed he was being beaten in prison because the warden and his sidekick wanted to get their hands on the stolen money. Even talking about the things that happened to other convicts behind those walls was something Hadley would not want. The old adage, *Where there's smoke, there's fire*, could start an unwanted invesitgation.

And Hadley, with his obsession about running a 'no-escape' prison, wouldn't want it known just how close Logan had come to getting away when Bird had helped him . . . It might give other inmates similar ideas . . .

Hadley would figure he had to nip that in the bud, pronto. Spilling a little extra blood to do it wouldn't trouble his sleep in any way.

So they had marked him down for death in the desert . . . Maybe Collie would have made one last try to find out about the bank money, but they were ready, even if reluctant, to let it go as long as Logan Breck's mouth was closed for good.

★   ★   ★

And now here he was on this train, a free man only because his death had been faked, and he had had a little luck, heading for Flagstaff, where, hopefully, he would learn the truth about what had really happened to Laurie.

And he would find that out, even if he — and others — had to die to do it.

7

'The Lord Helps Those Who . . . '

Warden Lester Hadley was no fool.

It didn't take him long to figure out that something had gone wrong out in the desert.

Collie should have reported in and been back here by now! *Long ago, dammit!*

He sent for Crow Delaney, a man who could be called Collie's understudy for he was just as brutal as the head guard, just as greedy, just as conscienceless. All attributes which Hadley could admire in his subordinates.

Crow was a big, dark, hulking man with a large face and head and practically no neck at all. He shaved regularly, although a shadow always darkened his heavy jowls. Curiously he let his hair grow shaggy, had it cut only randomly. It was jet black, black as the wings of the bird he had been named after. His eyebrows were heavy, like smears of charcoal, above deep sockets where yellow-green cat's eyes lived. These were usually expressionless — like now, but could turn coldly malevolent in the beat of a shoo-fly's wing.

'Outfit for a desert ride,' Hadley ordered bleakly. 'Something's happened to Collie.'

Delaney's face didn't change. 'Before or after he fixed Breck?'

'You find that out — I've a hunch Breck bested him.'

Crow scoffed. 'Sun might take a day off, too.'

Hadley's eyes narrowed. 'Don't make that mistake. Logan Breck is the hardest son of a bitch I've ever had inside these walls. Collie would've been in touch or back here where you're standing by now if things had gone according to plan — you go find out what happened.'

Crow knew that look and tone and

nodded hastily. 'Right, chief.' Crow fingered his six gun butt. 'I take it if I find the worst had happened and Logan's turned the tables on Col, I set things right?'

Hadley's eyes glittered. 'At any cost.'

'Speakin' of which: this bonus time I'm workin' on?'

Hadley hesitated, then nodded jerkily. 'All right. Bring me proof that Breck's dead and you've earned five hundred dollars ... otherwise, put it down to experience.'

Crow felt a strange wriggly kind of sensation in his chest. *Son of a bitch don't care a damn about Collie: only that Breck don't get away and blot his record.* Crow's tongue tip showed briefly as he licked his lips and said, 'OK, if that's the deal.'

'I'm not in the habit of repeating myself, Crow, you should know that. Hire extra men if you need them.'

Crow turned to the door, 'I'm on my way.'

About the time that Logan's train pulled into the depot at Flagstaff, Crow Delaney reported back to Hadley — with the worst possible news.

'Logan told that idiot sheriff in Papago Wells he was Collie, and the damn lawman believed him!'

'Well, he'd never met Collie so it was understandable, I guess,' Hadley said quietly, although his knuckles showed white through the skin where he gripped the arms of his desk chair. 'Why did he even bother reporting in to the sheriff . . . ? He could've skirted the town and made his run.'

'Wondered myself,' Crow said, putting on what he figured was a thoughtful expression. 'Asked a few questions and seems this sheriff, Wilde, had the papers for the judge who was gonna decide if Breck got a new trial . . . '

Hadley was way ahead, swore softly. 'So he got a look at those papers, told

126

the sheriff he couldn't hang around, that he had to go on down to Fort Bigelow on my behalf and' — he arched his eyebrows — 'disappeared . . . ?'

Crow Delaney smiled thinly. 'Didn't figure it was worth wastin' time tryin' to find Collie's body — Logan had all his identification so he musta killed him. I picked up a trail, though, chief. Logan's headed for Flagstaff. It's mentioned in them papers — the lawyer the gal hired is there and . . . '

Hadley's fist crashed onto the desktop and he thundered, eyes bulging, 'Then what in *hell's* name are you doing back here?'

Crow tugged at an ear lobe. 'Well, chief, there is a way to bring Logan out of hidin', a certain sure way . . . '

Hadley looked doubtful but said, 'I'm all ears . . . '

★   ★   ★

There was no help from the lawyer, a hard-eyed and tight-lipped man with strands of steel-grey showing in his hair and sideburns, name of Ingleheim. A cold unfeeling type, with a superior attitude. 'You claim to be Miss Laurie's uncle, correct?'

Logan nodded, weary and stiff from the long train journey. He stifled a yawn. 'That's right — Larry Carson. Her mother married my brother, a cattle agent of some standing.'

'I know the late Mr Carson's reputation — but I never heard he had a brother. You are not mentioned in his will as a beneficiary, or in any other way.'

Logan shrugged. 'We didn't get along all that well. I'm a drifter and he didn't like that. Look, I'm not after a share of any money or anything like that, I just want to trace Laurie, or find out what happened to her.'

Ingleheim arched his eyebrows. He spoke carefully in that lawyer manner, choosing his words as he did so. 'I can't help you. A client's privacy is sacrosanct. You have no proof to back up your interest in this. So, I'm afraid we're both wasting each other's time — and *my* time is precious. My clerk will show you out. Good day, sir.'

Logan stood now. 'I didn't come here to be passed-off with a lot of horse manure! You've got information I need . . .'

Ingleheim sighed in exasperation. 'Mr Carson, I am unable to help you. I thought I'd made that abundantly clear. I have no instructions from Miss Laurie to divulge any information to you or anyone else. Until I receive such instructions . . . ' He spread his clean, white hands with their even, smooth nails and half-smiled meaninglessly.

'I don't see how you can hope to receive instructions from someone I believe to be dead.'

For an instant something flickered across the lawyer's pinched face. 'I have no idea why you should believe that. I have no information one way or another. Now.' Somewhat impatiently, he tugged the bell cord beside his desk and moments later a skinny clerk opened the door and poked his head inside anxiously. 'Mr Carson is leaving, Wilson.'

The clerk looked even more anxious when he regarded Logan in his dusty old clothes and saw the holstered six gun in its tied-down holster. The man's stubbled face was hard, even mean-looking. Obviously Wilson didn't fancy his chances of physically removing Logan from the office.

Logan gave the lawyer a sour look and took pity on the nervous clerk. The man jumped back in alarm when Logan touched him lightly on the shoulder. 'Go back to your books, sonny, I can find my own way out.'

The clerk looked so relieved he almost bowed as Logan stepped past him into the outer office.

He left Ingleheim's door open behind him and heard the lawyer snap harshly at the clerk to close it at once.

He went easily enough, without fuss. Because he knew he would be back.

After dark.

The office was closed down when Logan returned at around ten o'clock that night, the entire place in total darkness and deserted.

Just the way he wanted it.

The knife he carried in his boot top was more than just a hunting tool. It was a fine skinner and would hold an edge through constant hard use from moon-to-moon. The back of the blade was eighth-inch thick tempered steel and the spear point tapered symmetrically.

It slipped easily between the edge of the rear office door and the frame. A little sideways pressure, a creak or two as screw threads strained against old timber fibres. Then metal struck metal as the blade met the lock's tongue, which was brass, a much softer metal than the knife's tempered steel. The edge cut a nick in the brass with hardly any pressure, a twist of Logan's wrist and the blade bit in — and moved the tongue out of its socket. His shoulder pressing against the door panel did the rest.

He sheathed the knife and closed the door carefully behind him. It didn't fit so well but on the way out he would give it a hard yank and it would thud into place, the tongue would spring back into the lock and the only sign of his entry would be a little paint scratched off the jamb. He would be long gone before they discovered it, for this was Saturday and there would be no work tomorrow. Even on Monday, they might put it down to some drunken cowboy just out for a little mischief.

He had noticed heavy drapes on the windows in Ingleheim's office when here before and he made sure these were pulled firmly across, overlapping so no chinks of light would show. Then he lit a desk lamp, took it to the tall filing cabinet, looked at the lock and returned to the desk. The knife blade opened the only locked drawer easily and inside he found a ring of keys, one of which fitted the filing cabinet door.

In ten minutes, he was reading the file marked, *Carson, Miss Laurie — Confidential — To be opened ONLY by The Principal.*

Logan shook his head, smiling crookedly: these high-priced legal people sure liked to strut and give themselves fancy names. *Principal? Principal what? He reckoned he could think of a couple of things — if he had time.*

He sat at the desk with the lamp turned low and opened the file, straining to make out the words and to understand the meaning. He wished he could read better.

He was there a lot longer than he intended and still wasn't sure he savvied all of what the papers said. Mostly it was a reiteration of Logan's story and his arrest and conviction on what was essentially circumstantial evidence bolstered by his past record. No one seemed perturbed about this, except Laurie. A firm hand which he guessed to be Ingleheim's had marked in the column next to Logan's story *Justice has been served.*

Which didn't sound too hopeful to Logan, but reading between the lines, Laurie had apparently worked her charm on the stoic Ingleheim and he had agreed to collate the facts and pass them on with his recommendation to the local Chamber of Justice for consideration of a new trial . . . Logan wondered about that and then he found the explanation: a legal agreement between Laurie and Ingleheim. It gave the lawyer a right to keep forty per cent of any compensation paid to Logan Breck provided he was granted a new trial and found to have been wrongly imprisoned.

Logan swore softly. Ingleheim with his holier-than-thou attitude about keeping a client's privacy and sticking to the letter of the law was nothing more than a greedy shyster, milking as much as he could out of a young, inexperienced girl. Laurie would have readily agreed, of course. Money meant little to her when you got right down to it and she would have agreed simply because it gave Ingelheim added incentive to work harder on Logan's behalf. So she had signed the paper and . . .

The date was two weeks after the last mail call in the prison without any letter for Logan! Two weeks after the three months when he had finally believed she was dead!

'But if she was here, in this very office, signing this paper,' he murmured half aloud, 'she had been very much alive!'

Heart hammering, he silently added the corollary to that: *and she could still be alive — still — alive!*

The possibility took his breath away and filled his head with swirling, rioting thoughts.

Which distracted him.

So that when the door opened and the big shadowy figure with the gun in his fist stepped in silently, he was taken by surprise. 'Workin' kinda late, ain't you, feller?'

It was a deep voice, edged with arrogance. Logan's head snapped up and he was moving instantly. He scooped up the thick pile of loose papers in a single sweeping movement, sending them in a whirling snow-storm across the room. Maybe only half the papers reached the man in the door but it was enough to startle and distract him.

Logan was already around the desk and rushing through the flying papers which now filled the air. Some had not yet settled on the floor by the time he had charged through the snowstorm and rammed a shoulder into the other's chest.

The big man grunted and slammed into the door frame, slapping papers out of his face, bringing his gun up. Only to have it beaten from his grip by Logan's clenched fist. Another followed and cracked against the man's lantern jaw. He spilled through the doorway into the outer office, lit vaguely by light coming in through the windows from the street outside. Logan had hoped to drop the man cold and then make a run for it.

But now he had a tornado on his hands as the guard or whoever he was, came back swinging. Big, meaty fists shook Logan's frame as they hammered home. He twisted and ducked and weaved, got in under the man's guard and straightened as he drove a savage blow into the thick midriff. The man might have looked like he was fat but that was solid muscle around his waist and Logan knew he was in trouble when his opponent merely grunted, took a step back, but set himself for another swing. It might have taken Logan's head off had it landed, but he was quick enough — or maybe he stumbled on a loose coir mat underfoot at the right moment — to dodge and lurch to one side.

He struck the edge of a small desk, the wooden legs scraping loudly across the linoleum, the desk tilting. Logan got it between himself and the attacker. He shoved the desk hard and the man sagged across it as the edge drove into his lower belly.

Logan beat him on the back of the head, smashed his face into the woodwork. That slowed the man down and he started to slip back off the desk. Logan heaved and the man went down. Logan stepped in to kick him and make a run while he was gagging for breath — or even unconscious.

A big hand grabbed his swinging boot, yanked hard and Logan joined the man on the floor. In seconds they were grappling, rolling and kicking and elbowing and snarling as they wrecked the outer office furniture. Surely someone would hear this racket! Logan thought briefly, taking an elbow in the mouth and feeling his lips split. Then he rolled onto his shoulders, got his knees up to his chest as the man hurled himself upon him. There was a grunt as boots met the hard body and Logan straightened his legs violently, teeth gritted with the effort.

The big man flailed back, crashed into the wall, the back of his head slamming hard into the timber.

His knees sagged and he dropped. Logan scrambled up, staggered in, lifted a knee into the bloody face, grabbed a handful of sweat-slippery red hair and banged the man's skull into the wood again. He stepped back and the intruder sagged forward, twisting onto his back as he fell and lay there, gasping, bleeding, fighting to stay conscious.

Logan was too damn exhausted to finish him right away and clung to the wall, fighting his own battle for oxygen and just a little more strength.

Shaking his head to clear it, his aching brain was just too slow to realize the man on the floor was fumbling at his boot top. As the danger seeped through his soggy consciousness, Logan straightened but froze in his movement towards his six gun as a twin-barrelled derringer covered him. The hand that held it shook a little but it was close enough for a fatal hit if the gun was fired.

Logan lifted his hands. 'Easy!'

'Easy be damned! You bust my teeth! I oughta shoot you where you stand!' The man's speech was slurred but he was already struggling to his feet, watched carefully by Logan.

'I only wanted a look at some files. Ingleheim wouldn't give me any info this afternoon, so, operating on the rule that the Lord helps those who help themselves . . . ' He ended with a shrug.

And was surprised to see the man with the derringer and the blood-streaked face almost smile. 'And the Lord help those *caught* helpin' themselves!'

'All right — what now? You a deputy?'

'Town patrol. Early on my rounds tonight or you might've been gone when I arrived.' The little gun jerked and both men stepped back into

Ingleheim's office where the lamp still burned on top of a low cupboard. The big man hitched a hip onto a corner of the desk and, still covering Logan, picked up the lamp with his free hand. He held it so the light washed over Logan's battered face.

He swore, startling Logan, straightened and held the lamp even closer. 'Goddam! I *know* you! You're — lemme see — Brett — no *Breck* — Logan Breck. You were doin' ten years hard when I was a guard at Big Mountain.'

Squinting in the dull light, Logan tensed, giving the man the once-over. And suddenly he remembered him.

'Cooper Willis. Head guard for a while but something happened between you and Hadley and Collie took over . . .'

Cooper Willis nodded gently, hard eyes watching Logan every second. 'That sadistic son of a bitch suited Hadley better . . . He fired me because I wouldn't pull some of the deals he wanted me to.'

Logan recalled the incident. Willis had been tough, but fair. He would give the inmates a break now and again and that wasn't the way Lester Hadley operated. He looked hard at Logan.

'I heard just recent that you were dead — killed while tryin' to escape in the desert. Figured you had more brains than to try a fool move like that, but a few years in that jail will make a man do loco things. Way I heard it, was Collie killed you. Blew your head off — '

'Well — someone lost their head, that's for sure.'

Once again, Willis almost smiled. 'That could be taken a couple of ways, which is likely how you meant it to sound. 'Course, I wouldn't expect you to admit to anythin' more, so we'll leave it where it is, but you better tell me how come I'm holdin' my hideaway gun on a dead man. OK? And I mean *in detail*! Lots of detail!'

8

Tangled Trails

Willis lived upstairs in the back of a rooming-house and they went there through the dark, deserted streets. At the far end, on the edge of town, a late-night saloon was still being patronized and the distant sound of a tinny piano drifted through the open window as Willis lit a lamp.

'Pull down the blind,' he said to Logan who obeyed, pausing once to look out on the sleeping town.

'Kinda quiet. I recollect Flagstaff being a lot more lively.'

Willis smiled, dabbing at a bleeding lip. 'That was before they made Dick Dandy sheriff.'

'Heard of him. That his real name?'

'As real as he'll tell you — five feet five and all of it dynamite. He'll kick my butt come mornin' when Ingleheim complains about the state of his office.'

'You don't sound too worried.'

Willis shrugged. 'Just makin' beer an' travellin' money. Gonna head for the Dakotas. They need a town marshal in Deadwood and I figure I can get the job.'

'If it's still anything like it was when I was up there last, you'll earn your keep.'

'With Chance Foran's Wild Bunch, weren't you?' Willis was serious now, his eyes steady on Logan's battered face.

'Yeah. Long time ago.'

'Four, five years as I recollect. Before they put you in Big Mountain. You lookin' for Chance now?'

Logan gave him back the stare levelly. 'I'm looking for Laurie Carson — my daughter. I thought she was dead but — '

He told Willis how he had found her signature on the paper in Ingleheim's office. 'The date was three and a half months after I had her last letter. I believed all that time she must be dead.'

Willis was silent for a time, then said slowly, 'Hadley figured you knew where that bank money was stashed or where Chance was holed-up. He held back the girl's last few letters, hopin' he'd find somethin' in them to help him locate the money, or Foran himself . . . '

Logan swore. 'The son of a bitch! He let me think — *told* me! — Laurie had died!'

Willis shrugged. 'Typical Hadley. I left about that time. Knew you'd be in for a taste of hell. Hadley don't let go of a chance to fill his pockets easy . . . You try to bust out before they took you into that desert?'

Logan told him about his attempts to get through the Big Mountain wilderness and almost making it, his ill treatment after, and finally Hadley's decision to kill him in the desert and mark it down as 'shot while trying to escape'.

Willis studied Logan, nodded gently. 'Hadley kept quiet about your last escape attempt — you're the only one I know could've pulled it off. You find anything in Ingleheim's papers that'll help you locate the gal?'

Logan said nothing and Willis broke in impatiently, 'Come on . . . Ah, holdin' back, eh?'

'Mebbe so, mebbe not. What's your interest, Willis?'

After a short pause, Cooper Willis said, 'Long ways to Dakota and if I get that job, I'll have to work my butt off, maybe get myself killed, in a helltown like Deadwood. If there's easy money floatin' around, up for grabs, I ain't too proud to have a crack at findin' it.'

'You think I'll help you do that? Listen, Coop, what I told you and what Laurie wrote in those legal papers was the truth: I was nowhere near the Dogwood bank when it was robbed. I just wasn't able to prove it. All I wanted from Foran on the train was what I'd had deposited in my account.'

'Uh-huh.'

'Ah, the hell with you! I don't care whether you believe me or not. It ain't gonna make any difference one way or t'other. I dunno where Chance is, or the money, which, it's my private guess, he's spent long ago. I just want to find my daughter.'

Willis was silent while he rolled a cigarette, licked the paper awkwardly because of swollen, split lips, then tossed the makings to Logan. While the man built his own cigarette, Willis lit up and said, 'Somethin' you dunno about that bank money — it was ranch cash, trickled in over the months in dribs an' drabs, from small deals or poker winnin's — all denominations, built up fast. The bank, being tidy like most banks, wanted to put those hand-size notes back into general circulation. They totalled 'em up, then exchanged 'em and made up the deposit in hundred-dollar bills, with a few smaller ones, maybe, make it right — and they were *new* hundred dollar bills.'

Logan frowned. 'I didn't know that, but what difference does it make? It was still fifty, sixty thousand or whatever was stole, even if it was in cents and nickels.'

'New hundred buck bills, I said which means they had consecutive numbers and were recorded.'

Logan lit his cigarette, blew smoke, still looking puzzled. 'Yeah, I've heard they've traced stolen money that way before, but hundred dollar bills ain't the oddity they once were, specially in trail towns. No one pays 'em too much heed these days. Might raise an odd eyebrow over the counter in a general store but that's all.'

'Maybe true in the bigger towns but they're still scarce, even in places the size of Flagstaff — so anyone pays with a hundred buck note will get it noticed. Even if the number's not picked up, which it wouldn't likely to be now, the bill and who offered it'll be remembered and that'd be too risky for Foran. But, if he's as cunnin' as I recall, he'll have had that loot stashed away until it was safe to bring it out and start spendin' . . . Three, four years would be about right. And that's how long it's been since the Dogwood robbery, ain't it?'

'Hadley would know that about the hundred-dollar bills?' At Willis's nod, Logan's mouth tightened. 'So that's why he put the pressure on me again — figured it was time to collect and I'd try to escape and meet up with Foran and collect my share.'

'Maybe, but he'd also be worried about his reputation and you havin' almost made it off Big Mountain with that Injun. He'd see it as an incentive for someone else to make a try, and possibly pull it off. So he was willin' to pass up a slice of the loot just to shut your mouth permanent so's his record of 'no escapes' would stay intact.'

'Hell, is he that loco?'

'And then some. But forget Hadley — what didn't you tell me you found in Ingleheim's papers?'

Logan smoked slowly, silently. Willis waited a minute or so, then his battered face hardened. 'I turn you over to Dick

Dandy, friend, and you ain't never gonna get a chance to look for your daughter.'

Logan snapped his head up, eyes narrowed, reading the other's set face correctly: Cooper Willis wasn't joking.

He sighed. 'There was this old Indian in the hills when I was trapping mustangs — just about the time Foran pulled the bank robbery in Dogwood.'

'If you were thinkin' some judge'd take the word of a smelly old Injun you met in the woods, you're ready to write a letter to Santa Claus come Christmas!' Willis scoffed but stopped suddenly. 'Aaah! You knew they'd never believe the Injun, din' you? That's why you never even mentioned him at the trial.'

'Figured, like you, that no court would take the word of a wandering Cheyenne medicine-man by way of an alibi for me. And it would look like I was grasping at straws, making it up, so I never mentioned him. Anyway, he probably wouldn't've testified, even I could've found him. I didn't do much for him: just set his broken leg after his horse died under him. He stayed a few days while I saddle-broke a mustang for him. Then set out for his tribe's camp, or in the direction he said it was. I don't think he'd trust a white man by telling him the real location.'

Willis was leaning forward now. 'You *helped* him! You never said that before!'

'Makes no difference. It was nothing much and he never even thanked me — which is the Indian way, any-how . . . '

Willis looked mighty thoughtful then. 'I dunno, some of these Injuns, 'specially the older ones, feel beholden, even to a white man, if you do 'em a favour. You likely saved the old coot's life! There's a chance he just might've convinced a court you were nowhere near Dogwood. If you'd brought him in.'

'Thought of that but his bunch were nomads. They never leave a sign to show where they've been or where they're headed. The way they been hunted down, can't blame 'em, I guess.'

'Well, we'll leave that. But you saw somethin' in those papers tonight, didn't you?'

Logan was reluctant to answer but finally nodded. 'Last thing I wanted to read — in one way. In another it told me that there was a good chance Laurie was still alive . . . '

'She went lookin' for the old Cheyenne?'

'Yeah. You believe it? Just a kid, not yet eighteen, alone, riding through Injun country — to help me!'

'Guess she likes her old man.'

Logan sounded truly puzzled when he said, 'But why, Coop? I've never been able to do anything for her! All she knows about me is that I'm a drifter with a touch of outlaw and a jailbird to boot. Yet she — she — ' Words failed him.

'You're her father,' Willis said simply. 'Her *real* father. That's what it comes down to and that makes her a mighty

152

fine young woman, Logan, carin' about you. You got any brains at all, you'll do your damndest to find her.'

'Christ, I'll try! But where the hell am I gonna start looking? Where the hell is *she* looking?'

'She might've picked up a clue you know nothing about. Anyway,' he added, eyes flickering, 'I can help you.'

Logan blinked. 'You?'

'Uh-huh. I'm somethin' of a drifter, too, had a hundred jobs, two hundred. Scouted for the army a spell in seven different States an' Territories. And I've come across plenty of nomad Injuns who never stay put for long, afraid of bein' hounded or attacked by us — trustworthy whites.'

Logan scarcely dared breathe. 'You figure you could track down that tribe with the old medicine man? Hell, it's a couple hundred miles from here and three years back down the track!'

'Mebbe so, but these wanderin' Injun groups, they follow the same trails year after year. Arrive at, say, Painted Horse

153

Canyon each spring, move on to Twin Rivers for the summer, south to Saddleback for fall, then hole-up for winter in some tight little box canyon that'll give 'em shelter from the snow and winds. Afterwards, it's on the trail back to Painted Horse — and so on. Not always a strict timetable and sometimes they'll head off to someplace new, but there's a general pattern. So, gimme a name, and a good description: it might be enough so's we'd have a pretty fair chance.'

'Called himself U-sha — *OO-shay*. Drawn out. He had a triangle of red-coloured bird bones woven into one of his hair braids. I know it's some kinda totem for a medicine man, but I've heard that it can indicate which tribe, too.'

'Yeah!' Willis sounded mildly excited. 'And that one, the red triangle of bird bones, probably from a sagehen, and coloured-up with ochre or plant dye — the red means he comes from a breakaway group, and I think they call themselves *Sheo sha*. Logan, we're already on our way! I know the circuit that lot follow!' Then he sobered. 'Too late for you to try and clear your name, of course, but then you don't have to! Long as folk believe you're already dead.'

'The hell with clearing my name! The hell with Chance Foran and his bank loot, too! All I want to do now is find Laurie.'

'Sure. Find the Injuns and we'll pick up Laurie's trail.' Willis said confidently, then stopped and his eyes changed, hard and bleak. 'An', sure, you forget about clearin' your name — you've lived with the outlaw tag for years so what the hell? But' — his gaze tightened even more — '*don't forget about Foran. And his loot*! Because that's what *I'll* be after and I'll need your help to do it. Just like you'll need mine to trace the gal. So, we got a deal? Or we gotta fight some more?'

Logan smiled wryly. 'I've had enough fighting.' He held his hand out without

155

hesitation and they shook on it.

Now all they had to do was unravel the tangled trails and see where they led.

★ ★ ★

The telegraph message was delivered by a special messenger who carried all such communications to Big Mountain Penitentiary.

He was Curly Sabato, a weathered, tobacco-chewing ex-Pony Express rider who would rather spend a week crossing a desert than sit around a depot waiting to deliver a wire to someone in town or at a ranch that was no more than a couple of hours' ride away.

Hadley knew him, disliked him because he smelled and wore buckskins that he must've had since the days of the defunct Pony Express. But the man would hang about in case Hadley wanted to send a reply: so the warden sent him down to the stores section with a chit that would allow him to consume up to four large whiskeys while he waited. No more.

Then he sprinkled a little cologne around the office and read the wire. It was from Crow Delaney in Flagstaff.

Traced him to here. Left town with an old friend of ours — Cooper Willis. Outfitted for long trails.
Waiting for your instructions.

'Damn fool!' Hadley said aloud, crumpling the message. 'Can't you think for yourself!'

Angrily, he drew a pad towards him, picked up a pencil and wrote swiftly, scratching out a word here and there, to replace others. The final message read:

Follow: Complete assignment with all haste. Use alternative plan if main target lost.

He hesitated, then added,

Hire help if needed. Expenses covered.

Hadley sat back, chewing at his bottom lip as he read and re-read the message. 'Expenses covered'. He liked that! *They'd come out of Delaney's bonus but the man didn't need to know that.*

Then he pulled the bellrope beside his desk and the door opened almost immediately. A prison trusty stepped inside. 'Yesssir, Warden?'

Hadley held out the message form and the man strode across to take it.

'See that smelly old galoot leaves immediately with my reply. Give him a fresh horse if need be.'

The trusty hesitated. 'Don't think he'd take one, Warden. We've tried before, but he likes that old jughead with the one ear he rides, wore-out or no.'

Hadley smashed a fist onto his desk. 'Damnit, don't ask him! Give him a fresh horse! And tell the fool that message is urgent. If it's not sent at once, it's the last he'll ever deliver! You tell him that!'

'Sure, Warden, sure.' The man backed out hurriedly, nodding, muttering he would see to it right away.

Hadley lit a cigar and was surprised to find his hand shook a little.

This damned Logan Breck was starting to get to him and he didn't like it. The sooner the man was dead and buried — *for sure this time!* — the better he would feel.

Pity to pass up a chance at all that money, but his reputation and his future meant more to him than dollars. Riding on his past record he could be assured of a posting in an advisory capacity to the Justice Committee when his contract came up for renewal. *Very soon, too!*

Once there, the sky was the limit, and he would be Washington-bound, find himself a suitable wife, able to live in a decent society, with trained servants who knew their place, instead of stuck in the stench of this muck-hole, with only a lot of murderers and thieves and perverts. He smiled around his cigar.

Ah, yes! Washington Society with its culture and women in crinolines who smelled sweet and exciting. Exactly what he deserved! And he would have it all . . . soon!

'Very soon!' he allowed himself to mutter aloud and decided it definitely called for a drink, worthy of such an occasion. He opened a cupboard and brought out a sealed and dusty bottle of Napoleon Brandy, taken a year ago from some cross-eyed Mexican smuggler who could never appreciate such fine quality.

Savouring the moment, he poured a ringing crystal goblet half full, sniffed the aroma and sat back to enjoy it.

Hadley regarded himself as a victim — a victim of political enemies who had had enough clout to have him sent to this penitentiary posting for five years — never believing he would endure.

'But I've beaten you all!' he said

aloud, holding his goblet to the window light, watching the mellow fire move through the liquid. 'I've not only endured, I shall be rewarded. Five years tenure up in a few more months and a spotless record: not one successful escape in all that time! No one else has ever come near such a record. I will certainly be promoted to the Judge Advocate's Committee and, my *dear friends*, you had better watch out!' He chuckled and said in a stage-villain's voice, 'For I am a vengeful man!'

He tossed the brandy down in one huge gulp.

9

Blood on the Pueblo

They had covered a lot of trails in the past two weeks but had found no sign of the Cheyenne medicine man or his band of nomads.

Staring at the map, Cooper Willis who was chewing on a pine sliver so as to cut down on tobacco which by this point on the trail was in short supply, tapped the crinkled, creased paper.

'You know where we been ridin'?' he asked Logan who was frying the last of their sowbelly with beans. They had been nibbling at this for four or five days, and the grease smelled so bad that a coyote had turned up his nose at a piece of beef Logan had fried in it and tossed to him the night before.

'I know *how*. Just have to move and

feel my spine creak and my backside start aching.'

'Well, we might've pushed things a little.' Willis turned the map towards the fire so the light of the flames flickered across it. 'See this?' He tapped the paper four times.

Logan recited slowly. 'Arizona, Utah, Colorado and New Mexico — their boundaries all meet in the one place, only common point where four states touch — We've been in parts of 'em all, last couple weeks . . . what's your point?'

'Little far west for the Cheyenne, ain't it? Even nomads don't usually stray this far from home ground.'

Logan frowned, flipped over some bacon, set the pan at the edge of the small fire. 'I've run across 'em up in Utah.'

'How big a bunch?'

'Aw — four or five. Just a family.'

'Yeah! You can find half-tamed Piute families up along the Green River, too, in Wyoming. Or Arapaho, even

163

Comanche — *but just the odd one or two!*' Logan frowned at the note of excitement rising in Willis's voice, and the man asked, 'He tell you he was Cheyenne?'

'U-sha? Yeah — no, wait! He didn't say anything while I was setting his broken leg. You know how they are. Silent, turning in on themselves to avoid thinking of pain and such. I just ran through the names of a few tribes and when I mentioned Cheyenne, he kinda grunted. Might've been from a twinge of pain, but I took it he was saying yeah, he was Cheyenne. Why?'

Willis nodded. 'He have any turquoise on him? Danglin' round his neck, sewed into his clothes, or hair . . . ?'

Slowly, Logan nodded. 'He had a piece like an upside down triangle set in silver, on braided strands, like an armband, way up high on his bicep. Something you wouldn't normally see under his clothes, but he had to take off his shirt so's I could bind his bruised ribs. That's when I saw the armband. Mean something?'

'Could be!' Cooper Willis slapped the back of his hand against the map and spat out the sliver of pinewood. 'I reckon your medicine man was Navajo, not Cheyenne.'

Logan pursed his lips. 'He could've been — had a broader face than a Cheyenne, I guess. They still wander all over the south-west, don't they? Navajos? Hopis . . . ?'

'Yeah — visiting the old *pueblos*, stayin' in touch with their ancestors, the ones they call the 'Anasasi', 'cause no one knows what their real name was . . . Settled this here country couple thousand years ago, and we're still findin' their *pueblos* built into cliffs, even some of their straw sandals, gnawed corn cobs, clay cookin' pots. 'Anasasi' means 'Savage People'. Apaches are s'posed to be descended from 'em.'

Dishing out the food, Logan asked, 'How come you know all this?'

'Worked as a digger for a team of archaeologists from a Boston Museum for a spell . . . '

Logan smiled thinly as he started to eat. 'How the hell did a man like you ever spend time working in Big Mountain Pen?'

'Was a guard's job vacant and I needed work — didn't suit me, though.' He swallowed, grimacing. 'Judas, that sow-belly's tough! I like to try different things, see how folk live, or used to live. I reckon come sun-up we should start checkin' out the old *pueblos*. There're dozens here in this part below the Utah line, stretchin' east across Arizona into New Mexico 'It's worth a shot, ain't it?'

It was, Logan readily agreed.

Time was passing — and the longer it took for them to find some definite sign of Laurie Carson, the less chance there was of finding her alive. After all, a lone young white woman wandering through desolate, isolated country whose denizens were mainly wild animals and Indians none of whom had cause to like white people . . . Plenty of danger there.

'We'll skip breakfast,' Logan said suddenly. 'Ain't got much, anyway. Leave before sun-up.'

'This is country that'll break your back, Logan!' Willis pointed out, gesturing to the unseen rugged canyons and ravines and old water courses beyond the flickering firelight. 'I know you're gettin' impatient, but no sense in killin' ourselves — couple hours won't make a helluva lot of difference right now. Except we'll be able to see where we're fallin' down.'

He was right and Logan pushed back his eagerness to be riding and nodded. 'Yeah — OK. Soon as the sun touches that mesa rim, though, we ride.'

Willis smiled thinly — it was a slim compromise, but he had no real argument with it.

★   ★   ★

167

There was this huge red rock basin, sweeping for miles, dotted with broken crags and little cones with sagging tops or broken bases. Rock chips were everywhere, giving the horses hell for their shoes were working loose. They were forced to stop and use their gun butts to drive in the worn, loosened nails, tightening the shoes a little.

'Flint and lava,' Logan said, straightening stiffly, his reddened gaze raking the shattered walls and crumbling rims. 'We're down in an old volcano.'

'Yeah,' agreed Willis, wiping his face with a sodden, gritty bandanna. 'A million years since it last erupted, I reckon.'

'Hope you're right!' Logan squinted, lifting to his aching toes. He pointed into the deep shadow cast by a high cliff. 'There! Right at the base, just barely visible — jumble of old *pueblos*.'

Looking, Willis nodded. 'That's where they always built, deep back, base of the highest, hardest cliffs, ready to defend themselves to the death.'

'What the hell were they afraid of? I thought they owned this country . . . '

'Them archaeologists claimed they don't know what it was scared the Anasasi, but their places were sure damn hard to get at — either from above or below when some were built under massive rock overhangs. They made sure they could defend 'em properly.'

'Seen one in Colorado once. Matter of fact, was Chance Foran showed it to me. We used it for a hideout till the posse looking for us gave up.'

Willis had his field-glasses up to his face now. His shoulders tensed. 'By God! There's — there's someone there!'

Both men's voices were hoarse from the dust and the need to ration their meagre water supply. But there was an edge of excitement that Willis couldn't disguise: this was the tenth pueblo they had checked, the first they had seen with any signs of life, more recent than a few hundred years, that is.

There was a coloured Navajo blanket

caught on something at one of the gaping black rectangles that served as windows. There were not many of these: mostly what light reached the interior of the mud-and-stone buildings came from a trapdoor in the roof. The ladders used to reach such trapdoors were pulled inside with the occupants each night.

'That blanket's nowhere near a hundred years old,' Willis said slowly. 'From here, I'd say it was airin' after bein' slept on last night!'

'Let's go find out!'

Logan was already spurring away as Willis cased his field-glasses without hurry.

They were good glasses and he had quite easily made out the geometrical designs and stylized figures, human and animal, on the colourful blanket.

He had also seen the large bloodstain across one corner and running up to the unbound edge . . .

He loosened his rifle in the saddle scabbard before spurring after Logan

Breck who had drawn twenty yards ahead already.

It was built like other *pueblos* they had checked out: toe-holds in the rockface, now weather-worn, originally camouflaged so any stranger would not find them easily. And, oddly, something that even the archaeologists couldn't explain: the buildings were at least a mile from the land that was cultivated for growing their crops, almost certainly corn and maize and a few varieties of bean; the water source, in a permanent natural well, was three miles distant and each day the women would have to make the journey, fill their decorated clay pitchers, and bring back water for the crops and household use. Each night they all had to climb the rockface so they could enter the stifling buildings from the top through the small trapdoors.

Whoever or whatever the Anasasi had been frightened of, must have been a terrible enemy . . .

But there had been a more recent

enemy here before Logan and Cooper Willis arrived.

Bullets had pocked the walls, gouging the ancient adobe, exposing straw medium that hadn't seen sunlight in hundreds of years. One or two of the protruding lodgepole supports had also been splintered, irregular wounds showing starkly against long-weathered wood.

Both men had their rifles out now, stepping over glittering spent cartridge cases. Logan picked one up. 'Winchesters.'

'Mite modern for the Anasasi. Was your medicine man armed?' Then answered himself immediately, 'No, I s'pose not.'

'Knife only — aw, hell!'

Logan fell sprawling as he slipped while making his way over the rounded sandstone. He slid all the way back and had to start again. Willis drew ahead and had lowered himself down into the dimness of the narrow building by the time Logan reached the trapdoor.

Willis picked up a bundle of dried

reeds amongst smashed pottery and held a match to them. Smoke swirled and made them cough as they reached hurriedly for bandannas to cover mouths and nostrils.

Silently, they looked at the huddled bodies and the blood-splashed walls. Men and women, young and old, three children piled carelessly in one corner. All had been shot, some several times — no longer than a day or two earlier.

'Judas priest!' hissed Willis. 'Let's get out of here!'

The blanket Willis had seen fluttering in the breeze was in the next building. It had caught on a broken section of window ledge, a dead Navajo below. Blood smears showed where he had, with dying effort, pushed and jammed the blanket into a cleft, perhaps as some kind of warning to other nomads, or a last gesture of defiance to the men who had done this slaughter.

Among the bodies, Logan recognized U-Sha. The old man's chest bullet-smashed. Under the bloodstained, ripped buckskin shirt, Logan found the turquoise triangle armband that confirmed the dead man's identity.

'Logan.'

He spun round as Willis spoke in little more than a whisper.

The man was holding up a torn, checked, woman's blouse spotted with blood.

You could find a hundred like it in any general store on the frontier, but some gut-wrenching hunch told Logan just who it had belonged to.

10

'Whatever It Takes!'

It took them all day to get the bodies out of the *pueblo* and buried in the area they had prepared. Some, especially the children, were wrapped in blankets or cloth or hides that they found. Others just had to be laid down in the red earth and covered with more of the same.

Even though it was dark when they had finished, they made their way out of the redrock basin and camped on a small ledge. They turned in without eating nor speaking.

Next day they found the Navajo well amongst the rocks and filled their canteens, six in all, carrying three apiece. Most folk would allow that that was plenty, but in this sun-blasted country, the heat intensified by the rocky terrain, that water would have to be strictly rationed until they were within easy reach of another source.

Drink not the last mouthful till the Great Spirit reveals the next well . . . That was the old Indian adage.

Logan carried the section of bloodstained blouse in his saddle-bag. He had said little since they had found it. It could be Laurie's — had to be! It seemed logical, anyway.

Too damn logical!

As for the bloodstains — well, he didn't want to think about them. They could belong to the blouse's owner, or they might have splashed on it from a dying Navajo. *He refused to speculate beyond that . . .*

Cooper Willis shot a jackrabbit just before high noon and they ate it hungrily, even crunching the small bones for the little marrow they contained. The coffee was weak, the grounds having been used a couple of times already. Tobacco was way down now but they each rolled a slim

176

cigarette, sat in the shade and smoked.

'Seems your hunch was right,' Logan said after a while. 'She'd somehow tracked-down U-Sha and his people.'

'You can't be sure it was her . . . ' Willis started, but one bleak, up-from-under look from Logan cut his words and he nodded curtly. 'Yeah. No use foolin' ourselves, I guess.'

'None at all.'

Logan stood, massaging his aching lower back, stiff and sore from long riding and digging the mass grave in that sun-toughened soil. The sun was still low, had cleared the rimrock, and moved now between two broken mesas. The slanting rays threw distorted shadows and outlined an old watercourse that likely still flooded once in a long while, when there was sufficient rain back in the faraway green hills.

But the way the coarse sand lay amongst and against the rocky sides told Logan no water had flowed through here in a long, long time. Then he stiffened.

If that was so — and he knew damn well it *was!* — then what was that churned-up dark smear winding through the otherwise undisturbed paleness of the creek bed . . . ? It was broken, pocked, but the low shadows seemed to merge it into a single dark snake across the long-deposited coarse sediment.

'Coop, I think we might've found the trail of those murdering bastards!'

He was running for his saddled mount even as he spoke, taking Willis by surprise. He tightened the cinch-strap he had loosened to give the horse more ease, hit the stirrups and was going down off the ledge in a reckless half-slide, half-ride before settling properly in the saddle.

Willis ran for his own mount, leaving their gear, and by that time, Logan was skidding into the old creek bed, rifle in hand as he quit leather while the horse was still sliding to a stop. He turned his dusty, stubbled face towards Willis as the man joined him. Logan's eyes were bright and his dry, cracked lips pulled back in a rictus of a smile.

'They'd take this way because it's easier on man and horse. Six or seven riders — one a lot lighter than the rest.'

Willis snapped a look at him: he knew what Logan was saying. That lighter rider might be the girl . . .

Cooper examined the churned sand and by dropping to his belly and squinting along the twisting line of the shadow, he could just make out the slight difference in the colouration. A slightly deeper shade confirmed that it had been disturbed fairly recently — but with this kind of country it would be useless to hazard a guess as to *how* recently.

He sat back on his hams, thumbed his hat up off his face. 'Looks like the bunch — comes from the right direction.'

Logan's face was tight with excitement now. 'Going in the right direction, too.' Willis's glance was puzzled and Logan answered again with that tight grin. 'Making for the next water-hole.'

'You know where it is?' Willis was genuinely surprised.

'Know where it ought to be.' Logan pointed to distant, low hills, slightly to the right of where they stood. 'Creek's course would run between those hills, maybe even start there. It's the kinda place you find a small well or natural tank, hard in against the wall that throws the most shadow.'

Willis nodded: he knew his wilderness lore well enough to agree that what Logan said was so, though there wasn't always a water-hole in such places. But the signs were right and these men they were trailing would naturally make for it, hoping to find fresh water.

This kind of raw, killer country actually dictated the way a man with some savvy of the wilderness would have to ride. *He would have to look for water in the most likely places, whether he found it or not . . . if he wanted to survive, he would have to go where water was supposed to be.*

'Better get our gear,' Willis said,

turning back to his horse.

Logan was already moving, leaping into the saddle of his weary, dusty, thirsty grulla.

They stayed away from the creek bed, keeping to the broken rocks either side, crossing over when the other offered better cover, though not necessarily easier riding.

The horses suffered. It worried both men who, like true, wise and experienced drifters, treated their mounts humanely and thoughtfully, knowing their lives depended on their welfare. This slowed them down and it was almost sundown before they were within spitting-distance of the break in the hills.

Cautiously, they slowed even more, chasing the shadows, searching for sand patches underfoot to avoid making noise.

And just as well they did.

Logan smelled the woodsmoke first, signed to Willis, and they set their mounts behind a screen of egg-shaped boulders. There was a glow in the pass, an early camp-fire. But something wasn't quite right . . .

'They're not camped on the side where the waterhole would be — if there is one!' Logan said quietly. It was natural for travellers to camp beside the water source. Even if it wasn't there, men had a habit of making camp where they had expected to find water anyway. 'The fire's a decoy.'

'Yeah, they're waitin' for us!' Willis hissed back, unlimbering his rifle and pulling off the old kerchief he had wrapped around the action to keep it as free of dust and grit as possible. Logan had done the same and now pulled the cloth off his own rifle's action, blowing on it gently to free it of any residual grit that just might cause a jam in either lever, cartridge-feed or ejector.

'Yeah, we see the fire, head that way. Likely silhouetting ourselves into the bargain . . . make fine targets.'

'Some smart *hombre* over there — Crow, most likely.'

'Who?'

'Crow Delaney: you oughta know that son of a bitch.'

'Sure — Collie's understudy! But why him?'

'He's part Injun. Where he gets the name, I guess. And I reckon by now Hadley would've sent someone to look for Collie . . . Crow'd be the best man for that.'

'Whoever he is, he's dead.'

'Better watch for the gal . . . ' Willis let the rest trail off at a glance from Logan. 'Sorry — 'course you will.'

Logan gestured with the rifle. 'You make through those rocks, I'll go this way — try to angle in so we can see both sides — it's narrow enough.'

'Yeah! Like fish swimmin' into a trap!'

'Pretend you're a shark — smash the trap and kill anything that moves within reach.'

Willis nodded. *Yeah. These butchering bastards deserved to die, whoever they were . . .*

He started to voice the thought but Logan had already moved off, lost now in the deepening gloom as he threaded his way through the boulderfield.

* ★ ★ ★

They had set it up well enough.

Not only had the killer band built their decoy fire, but they had dumped some of their gear and scattered a few blankets around to make it seem like a regular campsite. One bedroll even looked as if someone was sleeping in it, but was likely stuffed with dead foliage or heaped sand.

The men were actually hidden opposite, in the deep, dark shadow of the overhanging rock, where the water-hole would be, naturally screened from the heat of the sun.

The horses would be behind that huge rock that squatted like a giant toad on the land. If it wasn't for the girl — *he was certain-sure Laurie was there!* — he would make his way around and shoot the mounts. Or at least run them off.

He didn't aim for any of these killers to escape. If their mounts were dead, or lost, they would fight all the harder but — it didn't matter now, anyway. He couldn't take the chance. They would kill the girl if they thought they themselves were doomed.

The shot crashed and tore through the gloom like a thunderclap in the narrow pass, startling him enough so that he dropped flat instantly, and saved his life.

A split second slower and he would have died by that bullet. It splattered against the rock only a foot above his prone body and he felt the sting of hot, shattered lead through his shirt. Before he could move there were two more fast shots. His face was full of sand, grit crunching between his teeth, nostrils clogged. Luckily he could still see — and he saw the muzzle flashes of the rifle seeking him.

He rolled towards the shooter, taking

his body in closer to a low line of rocks, so that the man's next two shots skimmed the tops and ploughed into the sand beyond. The next chewed chips from the top of the rock above his head, the ricochet echoed and whined and seemed to take a long time to die.

Willis was targeted, too: several rifles were hunting them now. The killers had placed themselves up in the rocks on the dark side, making it an almost perfect ambush. Logan twisted onto his back, brought his rifle across his body and fired awkwardly. It was a lucky shot, apparently, for a man yelled in the darkness several feet up the large rock. Logan could make out the movement up there, blackness against dark grey. It was a difficult shot but his next bullet blew the man upright and he toppled down, rifle clattering. The gunfire paused briefly, no doubt the killers surprised by the hit.

Logan had pinned down two other places where he had seen muzzle flashes and while they were still stunned, he raked the area with hammering fire. The lead ricocheted and screeched and a man grunted, then yelled, a sob in his voice.

'Crow! He — he got me!'

No answer from Crow. But Willis's Winchester crashed in a prolonged volley and more lead hornets slashed through the gloom before guns opened up again from the rock slopes.

'I seen four!' Willis called softly, just as Logan fired once more.

'Three,' Breck answered, ducked and hugged the ground as lead chewed away the jagged rock just above his sprawled body.

It was duck and fire, duck and fire, risking the chance that the killers on the slopes would be waiting, trying to time their movements. But both Logan and Willis were old hands at this kind of thing, although Logan was somewhat out of practice. Still, instinct played a big part in it and they fired at random times, ignoring the occasional 'easy' shots offered by the enemy, knowing they were set-ups.

It was fully dark by now and harder for both sides to find targets. Willis called that he had been hit but it was just a graze. Logan had had his hat holed and another slug had seared his upper left arm, the bullet chipping wood from his rifle stock. But he was ready to fight on and knew at least two dead men lay sprawled at the foot of the big rock. A third was spread-eagled on the slope itself but he thought he heard moans and groans, though, later, there was silence and he had the impression that the man was no longer moving. Soon after the body slid limply to the bottom to join the others.

Logan grew impatient. There had been no exchange of words, just hot lead. He still didn't know if Laurie was there or not. Taking a chance, he flattened himself, lifted his head enough for his face to clear the sand and called,

'Laurieeee!'

That was all, repeated twice, before lead raked the shelter and he felt a rock chip slash at his left ear, the warm wetness on his neck telling him it had drawn blood.

'*Dad!*'

His heart seemed to stop as the single, brief word reached him — and he had the impression that it was deliberately cut off so that not even a small muffled cry followed.

He didn't answer. They might have let her call that one word in the hope he would speak up again and give away his position. But he couldn't speak even if he'd wanted to. She was there! *Not fifty yards away! Alive!*

Strangely, it wasn't as comforting as he had expected. Now he knew she was there, it only made him more wary. These were cold-blooded killers and she was their prisoner.

They would use her to make their escape now they knew who it was shooting at them.

No sooner had the thought formed than a voice he identified as Crow Delaney, confirmed by Willis, called down:

'We're goin', Logan! Takin' her with us! You fire one more shot, poke your nose out an inch, and she's dead. You hear me?'

'She dies, Crow, she'll have a lot of company.'

'Aw, we won't kill her right away! We can amuse ourselves with her for a while . . . But I'll leave a finger or an ear on a rock where you can find it.' There was a chilling laugh. 'And she's got ten fingers, ten toes, two ears, a couple of other things that could be hacked off. So I don't want to look over my shoulder and see a dust cloud anywhere! Might only be a sand-devil but I'll take it as bein' you — and she'll lose a bit more.'

Again that chilling laugh. 'Hardly be worth pickin' up, eh? So play it smart — stay put and don't follow. That way she stays in one piece — all up to you.'

To finish off his threat he did something that made Laurie scream, the piercing sound echoing through the darkness, churning Logan's guts.

Willis had to throw himself bodily at Logan and pin him down to keep the man from raging up and running towards the sound of Delaney's voice, heedless of risk to either himself or the girl.

'We have to let 'em go, Logan!' Cooper Willis gritted. 'We have to! I know Crow: he means every word.'

Logan groaned and forced himself to relax. Willis stayed with his weight pressed across him until they heard the horses beyond the big rock, moving away into the night.

'Four riders I make it,' Willis said quietly, 'Three of 'em men . . . '

There was no need for him to add that the fourth rider's horse made a softer sound because it carried a lighter load — like a young woman, instead of a beefy gun-toting killer.

'Get off me, Coop. We gotta figure out some way to get close enough to rescue Laurie without getting her maimed — or killed.'

'By God, Logan! I know it's gotta be

done, but, man, you are takin' one helluva risk!'

Logan's eyes were glinting in the darkness.

'Laurie's the one at risk. Anything I have to do to save her skin is nothing, Coop. *Nothing!* I'll kill 'em all and die doing it if I have to, but that gal is gonna be freed, whatever it takes!'

11

Hostage!

The four riders made it out of the worst part of the desert country by mid-morning. When they found a narrow, muddy creek, Crow Delaney decided they needed to rest the horses. No one complained.

Least of all Laurie Carson.

She was dishevelled, slumped in the saddle, her thin, raw wrists roped to the saddlehorn. Her hair was greasy, scattered twigs and wood chips caught in the strands. She was pale and gaunt, dark smudges under her eyes, much thinner than when she had last seen her father.

At the thought of Logan, she lifted her head slowly and turned to look over her shoulder, back into the shimmering heat haze from where they had come.

Come on, Dad!

'Yeah, he's back there someplace,' Delaney told her as he walked across, untied her hands and lifted her down easily. He grinned as he shook her lightly, hands almost meeting around her slim waist. 'You lost some weight, sweetheart! Din' them bad Injuns feed you proper?'

She strained against his grip, futilely, her pale blue eyes ablaze. 'Leave — me — alone!' she ground out. 'Those Indians treated me well! Far better than you and your — your pigs!' Then she smiled thinly. 'Not many of them left now, are there, I'm glad to say!'

He hit her, almost casually, the blow turning her head sharply to one side, hair flying.

'Hey, Crow, don't damage the merchandise!' called one of the riders, grinning ear-to-ear.

His companion, reloading a saddle carbine, laughed shortly. 'Little late for 'damage', ain't it?'

Laurie paled and felt her legs go

week. *Oh, no! Please God! Not again! Not these filthy animals pawing me — invading my body!*

She was almost physically sick at the thought, cringed when Crow Delaney reached for her. But he only chuckled as he dragged her to a patch of sand under some willows beside the small creek they had stumbled upon.

'Have yourself a bath. You'll feel better.' He laughed outright at her look. 'Hey, we won't look, will we, fellers?'

''Course not! Promise, sweetie!'

'Hell, Crow, we're *gennlemen*. No need to even ask!'

'There you are — go take a bath.' He pushed her towards the water and she stumbled, weak from her ordeal since these men had slaughtered the Navajos. 'You do it, or we'll do it for you.'

Breathing hard, she took off her moccasins, hitched up her fringed buckskin skirt — and walked knee deep into the water where she sat down and commenced to wash — first her hair, then her face, then reaching cupped handfuls of muddy water inside the blouse.

Crow laughed but the other two, Chuck and Boyd Lee, growled, looked at each other and began to wade out. 'Stay put,' Crow said, still chuckling. 'She's a smart cookie that one — did just what she was told.'

'You told her to take a bath!' growled Chuck, the taller of the brothers.

'And that's what she's doin' — with her clothes on. I never did say for her to take 'em off.'

Boyd growled, 'I'll take 'em off for her!'

Crow turned a cold look upon him. 'How many times you take off all your clothes when you wash?'

'Well, that's different . . . I mean . . . '

'Just leave her be,' Crow said, perversely pleased he had upset the brothers. They knew he was no man to mess with but they were bitterly disappointed. The girl, still wearing her sodden clothes, squeezed water from skirt and blouse as best she could, then sat on a rock in the sun, vigorously shaking her damp hair. She looked calm but, inwardly, she was trembling.

'You can be a damn spoil-sport when you want, Crow,' complained Boyd.

'Without even tryin'!' allowed Chuck. 'She gonna make us some coffee an' biscuits?'

'The hell you think this is, a goddamn picnic?' Crow had what the Lees called his 'Indian' look, a kind of tightening of his large features into a mean mask that could give young kids nightmares for weeks. The Lee brothers even found it unsettling. 'Brew your own coffee. Then draw straws or flip a coin and see which one of you stays behind.'

'What! Logan's back there! And that's Cooper Willis with him. He's no slouch. Hadley thought he was soft, but he ain't — I seen him when he was a deputy in Flagstaff, cut down two of Hank Mifflin's bunch and later blow Hank's knee cap clear off. Crippled him for life — I ain't about to get

197

within range of his guns again.'

'Sort it out between you,' Crow said coldly. 'And get it done quick — we pull out in half an hour . . . '

It did Laurie good to hear them squabbling among themselves. It gave her a little lift although she was already steeling herself for the ordeal she knew lay inevitably ahead for her. The brothers were the worst, Crow not bothering her unduly, but after Chuck had violated her, and he had beat the man for it, he seemed to think it was too late to be worrying much about her virtue any further. Still, he wasn't as troublesome as the others.

She hoped Chuck would draw the short straw and be left behind — although it made her afraid for Logan. The Lees were cold-blooded killers, had enjoyed slaughtering the young Navajo women, even the children.

Her stomach churned again at the memory of how Crow had led his band of killers in and methodically and coldly killed every Navajo. She had been sure she was going to die, too, but Crow had dragged her out of the corner where she had huddled and slapped her.

'Snap out of it, lady! You won't suffer no more at the hands of this scum!' His eyes had taken on a distant, almost glazed look as he added, 'Their mangy cousins, the Apaches, took my sister in a raid on our camp when I was a shaver and I ain't never forgot what they done to her — '

She had tried to punch him but she was still weak from the fever, sagged against him and said, voice muffled, 'They were *kind* to me, damn you! I was bitten by a snake and they found me near death lying in the desert, took me in and nursed me back to health. For weeks . . . They never harmed me in any way! *Now you've killed them all!*'

'I hope so. They ain't no loss. But you're our gain, lady. You can be worth a lot of money — and other things — to us.' He lowered his voice, adding, 'To me, anyways.'

And that was how it had started — *When, oh, when, would it end!*

★ ★ ★

Chuck lost the toss: he called tails when the battered half-dollar came down landing heads up.

Swearing, he asked Crow what he was expected to do.

'You ain't that dumb! Stop Logan, slow him down at least! Gimme a chance to get the gal away.'

'Hell, Crow, you seen what he done! We lost three men back there!'

Crow Delaney took a puff on his corncob pipe and stared coldly through the smoke cloud. 'Stop him — or slow him down. There'll be a bonus for you.'

'If we get back,' said Boyd with a tight grin, relieved it wasn't him who had to stay and ambush Logan Breck and Cooper Willis — yet vaguely sorry it had to be his brother. 'You gonna visit the gal before we pull out?'

'No he ain't!' snapped Crow and

Laurie, having heard, felt a slight, very slight, easing of the tension in her chest. 'We're movin' right now and that means you top-up your canteen, make sure you got enough ammo, and get ridin' into the pass. Don't try nothin' fancy. Just kill the son of a bitch from cover. Willis, too ... If you can't do that, shoot their hosses, but *you delay 'em!* You turn up and they're still comin', I'll shoot you myself.'

He threw a challenging look at Boyd and the smaller Brother Lee averted his gaze. He flushed, knowing he would never dare go up against Crow, even if the man did kill Chuck.

★   ★   ★

Because he had left the ambush pass so quickly and in the dark, Crow Delaney hadn't covered his tracks. So it was easy for Logan and Willis to pick up the sign and move along at a goodly pace.

'There's a creek somewhere up the way they're headed,' Willis said. 'Their hosses are thirsty enough they'll likely take 'em straight to it.'

'Well, we'll follow where the tracks take us but I'm hoping it'll lead us to a creek.' Logan shook his last canteen and the water slopped, sounding low. 'Need a refill.'

They were hot and thirsty and hungry but they didn't allow these things to distract them and by mid-afternoon they were closing on the fugitives' last campsite. Logan hauled rein as they approached a narrow pass through the hills and waited for Willis to come up alongside.

'Too many shadows in that pass for my liking — you know another way through here?'

Cooper Willis thought for a few moments and shook his head. 'Don't even recollect this pass. I wasn't this far west when I was here, more south . . . I'll go take a look.'

He swung his horse's head around and rode up the slope as far as a naked-looking bench. There was no brush, only a tuft of brown Austin grass growing amongst some heat-cracked rocks. Willis stood in the stirrups, flipped his reins to urge the horse on at a slow walk. He shaded his eyes and turned in the saddle to call down,

'Don't look like there's any other way, but the pass seems safe enough. Can see more light reflectin' down into it from this angle.'

'We-ell — still don't like it, but if you think it'll be OK we'll . . .'

Willis's horse jerked and started to fall sideways, the sudden collapse followed quickly by the sound of the shot. It was a dull crack without an echo and Logan knew it was fired from the rim of the pass, not down in the shadows where he had expected an ambusher to lie up.

There was a second shot and Willis, starting to jump from the saddle as the horse went down, suddenly spun in mid-air, his body twisted out of shape by the hammering bullet. He fell awkwardly. The horse was almost down now and rolled back across Willis's legs, pinning them.

But there was no movement from the man and Logan, rifle in hand already, spurred the bone-weary grulla down the short slope and into the lee of an eroded mushroom-shaped knoll which showed layers of different kinds of rock and sand. Bands of pink, yellow and grey.

Two bullets screeched off the rock above his head as he quit the saddle, slapped his hat across the grulla's rump and set it running on towards the pass.

If he was right about the bush-whacker being high on the rim, the man wouldn't be able to see the horse from his position. But he would hear it and, hopefully, would be concentrating on the narrow pass entrance where he would expect it — and its rider — to show.

Logan climbed the eroded rock mushroom swiftly, finding easy foot and hand holds. He slipped but kept the 'stem' of the mushroom between himself and the pass. Hat hanging down his back by the rawhide thong, he dropped prone and eased his head around the rough corner. He was right.

There was movement up on the rim right where he figured it should be as the bushwhacker moved into a better position to see the pass entrance.

At the same time, the man must have caught a glimpse of the riderless horse, realized he had been tricked. He flung a wild look around even as he thrust up, turning to run back under cover.

Logan's bullet knocked him clear off the rim and the man yelled once as he fell, bouncing down the steep slope of the wall into the pass. Logan clambered down fast, trotted after his horse which had stopped now to browse on a patch of the first really green grass it had seen in weeks. He gave the animal a swift pat on the rump, ran to where the bushwhacker lay.

The man was lying very still, badly wounded. Logan recognized him from his days of riding with Chance Foran.

One of the Lee brothers: killers and rapists and bloody-handed thieves from a clan that haunted the dangerous Pilgrim Trail along the northern section of the Red River. He seemed to be still alive, although there was a lot of blood.

Logan stripped him of a knife and a hideaway gun, saw the man's rifle had smashed its action during the fall, then hurried upslope to where Willis had gone down.

Logan approached slowly. 'Coop . . . ? You hurt bad?'

'Get this goddamn hoss off of my legs, dammit! My foot's gone to sleep!'

Logan smiled in relief and moved forward to see what he could do . . .

He had to dig away under the dead horse and then drag Cooper Willis free. The man writhed and threw his head side to side. He had been hit high up in the chest, on the left, but the bullet had passed through the breast muscle without damaging bone or cartilage. There was a deal of torn flesh, though, and plenty of blood. Logan washed the wound well with the last of his canteen water before binding it with Coop's spare shirt. It was bulky and it hurt the man to move his left arm but he said it felt better with something firm there. Logan rolled him a cigarette with a few remaining shreds of tobacco, made him comfortable in the shadow of the rock mushroom.

'I'll go have a word with Chuck Lee.' He indicated the sprawled, unmoving form of the killer down in the pass.

Willis was surprised. 'Thought he must be dead.'

'Not yet,' Logan said moving away and Willis frowned.

It wasn't Lee's lucky day: Logan aimed to get the last piece of information out of him before the man cashed in his chips . . . and he *would* die. Logan's bullet had taken him through a lung and he was coughing a lot of blood. Froth bubbled around his bitter, tight-drawn lips as Logan's tall shadow reached him. Standing against the sun, Logan looked down at Lee, who sneered back at him, hating him even now.

'You're all through, Chuck.'

'You bastard!' Lee choked, coughing again. 'Lemme alone! You — you've finished me . . . '

'Not quite.' Logan squatted beside him. 'You're dying, but there's still a helluva lot I can do to you to make your passing less than pleasant.'

Chuck Lee's wild eyes showed alarm. 'Lemme be!'

'I want to know about the girl.'

Lee stared back, eyes burning with a long hate, chest heaving, air whistling and bubbling through the wound. He coughed again, spraying blood. 'That gal! Man! I was the first . . . an' she — '

Cooper Willis had begun to doze but he awoke fully with a start that set his heart hammering as the wrenching scream rose from out of the pass. He struggled to sit up a little straighter, saw Logan, squatting, just pushing back from the wounded bushwhacker whose legs seemed to be kicking weakly.

'Judas priest!' Willis whispered.

After a while — and several more blood-chilling screams — Logan walked back, wiping his hands on a piece torn from Lee's shirt. He flung the red-smeared rag aside. His face was like a death's head as he stopped near Willis.

'Crow and Boyd Lee have still got Laurie with them. The bastards have been raping her regularly.'

'God almighty!'

Logan took a restless half-dozen steps around the dead horse, came back and stood in the same place as before, looking down bleakly at the wounded man.

'The *sons of bitches*!' He kicked a small rock in frustration, pulled down a deep, shuddering breath and stared off into the heat-haze for what seemed to Cooper like a long time. 'Is she still OK?'

Logan's head snapped around but he spoke carefully and more calmly now. 'She's still alive if that's counted as being 'OK' after what those bastards've done to her!'

'I only meant . . . '

'I know, Coop — I feel like tearing down the goddamn mountain but nothing's gonna do any good until I catch up with Crow Delaney.'

'Until *we* catch up with him.'

'I dunno, Coop. That wound of yours. The chest is tore-up pretty bad. Needs proper attention. There's a doc at a fort somewhere west of here if I recollect right . . . '

'Fort Harmon — been abandoned for the last couple of years.'

Logan arched his eyebrows. 'I never heard that.'

'Not the kind of news that'd be of much interest when you're inside Big Mountain Pen, I guess . . . '

Logan nodded slowly. 'OK — but that wound still worries me.'

'I'd be better without it,' Willis admitted, 'but I'll still ride with you after Delaney. I can use Lee's horse.'

Logan smiled slowly. 'Got it all

worked out, huh?'

Coop shrugged and wished he hadn't. The movement stretched the torn skin of the wound and he gasped, but covered quickly. 'We're gettin' into country I know if we're headed north — '

'North-west,' Logan corrected quietly and it was Willis's turn to arch his eyebrows.

'That's back towards Big Mountain!'

'Uh-huh — Laurie's Crow's hostage. But he needs somewhere to stash her.'

'Aw, you don't mean . . . ?'

Logan nodded. 'Lee told me Crow's taking her back to Hadley. If I want her back, I'll have to show up at Big Mountain.'

'And they'll kill you as soon as you're within rifle range!'

'They'll do that, if they can, wherever I show.'

Willis was feeling the strain now as shock set in and he had to struggle to form coherent thoughts and words. He seemed short of breath.

'Gettin' yourself killed won't do her any good.'

'No, but there's nothing else I can do but take a chance and go listen to Hadley's terms.'

'You already *know* what they'll be!'

'Like I said — nothing else I can do.'

It hurt, but Cooper Willis shook his head slowly. Then he stopped and tried to smile. It wasn't too successful but the effort was enough to put tension and expectancy in Logan's demeanour.

'Hadley's gonna keep her there inside the prison because no one can get at her, only on his say-so.'

Logan made an impatient gesture, 'Yeah, yeah, that's obvious . . . '

Again Cooper tried a smile and this time it was a little more successful.

'You ever heard of anyone tryin' to break in to a jail . . . ?'

12

Old Friends

After riding through the pass and starting across country that gradually gave way to some greenery and ever-thickening strands of timber, Logan could see that Willis was in real pain. He was running a fever, too, although he denied strenuously that he was.

His shirt was sodden with blood and that meant it had already soaked through the bulky layers of Coop's spare shirt. So he was losing a lot — too much.

There was no doubt the man needed a doctor, but in lucid moments Willis got so upset at the suggestion they ride for distant Kettle Creek, that Breck backed-off. But Willis's condition wasn't improving and he knew that sooner or later something had to be done . . . even if it meant delaying his pursuit of Laurie.

They were well back into Arizona by now, just north of the Black Mesa country where, according to reports, a new telegraph line was being laid. The heat was bearable, leastways, for a mostly fit man, but it played havoc with someone in Willis's condition. The man sagged drunkenly in his saddle but doggedly refused all offers from Logan to stop for a spell. So they pushed on, slowly, Logan keeping as sharp an eye out for a shaded waterhole as he did for an ambush set up by Crow Delaney.

It was punishing, lonely country and the distant hills and mesa did not seem to be drawing any closer. It was an illusion of course but Logan had to fight hard so that it didn't convince his tired, aching brain that it was necessary to take chances just to speed things along — like short-cutting across country even more waterless than this.

Laying down the law and calling an enforced stop, he boiled some of their precious drinking water, unwrapped the sodden bandages from Willis's wound and tried to keep his face straight as he saw its condition.

The flesh was swollen and enpurpled, with a thin film of pus already forming. Almost unconscious, Willis slumped as Logan cleaned the wound as thoroughly as he could and when he rebandaged it, he left a twist of cloth dangling to act as a crude drain for the suppurating wound.

This time, before starting out again, he roped Willis into the saddle and the fact that the man didn't even complain told Logan just how bad he must be feeling.

The Hopi Indians weren't giving any trouble these days so they didn't expect to meet an army patrol. But a little way to the south and east, sunlight blazed vividly from polished brass, the flash followed immediately by the plaintive, faintly audible notes of a bugle, sounding the alert.

Reining down, Logan reached out

quickly and steadied Coop in the saddle. The man was only half-conscious by now. Squinting against the glare and standing in his stirrups, Logan made out a reddish dust cloud and dark, moving specks below, strung out into two short lines, four or five riders in each.

'By God, that's a cavalry troop, all right!' Logan said, turning a puzzled face towards the sagging Willis. 'Thought you said Fort Harmon was closed down?'

'Last I heard — it — was.' Cooper Willis was gasping out each word now, slurring them together.

'Mighty cautious officer, dispersing his men that way . . . Indians must be giving trouble again.'

The troopers spread out in a shallow crescent, in case Logan or Willis tried to make a break for it. They were haggard and red-eyed, obviously having ridden a long trail. Soon they were in hailing distance and, in the shade of a granite overhang, Logan spoke with

Lieutenant Jonas Garnett. In his late twenties and obviously seasoned in wilderness patrol operation, Garnett was cautious, unbending ... and suspicious.

Playing it safe, Logan gave Cooper's right name but called himself 'Larry Carson'. Willis managed to fumble out some identification from his deputy job which was closely examined by Garnett. When Logan said he was just a drifter and had no real identification, except a letter from a rancher he'd worked for (and which Willis had written for him for just such an occasion as this) the officer seemed willing to accept it, mostly on the basis that Willis had recently been a deputy lawman in Flagstaff.

Twitching his sand-clogged moustache and taking in the way the men wore their guns and Willis's obviously poorly condition, Garnett asked, 'Indian trouble?'

Logan hesitated, not sure if this was some kind of trap. If Indian renegades were rampaging through country even as isolated as this, word would have spread like a brush fire. He was sure the Hopis hadn't broken their long-standing peace, so took a chance.

'Not Indians — whites,' he told the lieutenant. 'Outlaws, I guess, likely short of water and grub. Jumped us back there, near the pass, but we managed to drive 'em off.'

Garnett's blue eyes narrowed, his dusty, stubbled face pinched with interest. 'How many?'

If Garnett checked he would find the bodies of Crow's killers still lying out there, already feeding the vultures. 'Five or six — we accounted for three.'

The officer's face sharpened. 'By hell, that must've been a hot ol' time!'

'They were too eager — showed themselves on the slopes — and we're both good shots.'

'Need to be! Hunters?'

'Done some. That's why we're — '

Garnett interrupted, 'Your pard don't look too spry right now. That seems like a pretty bad wound.'

'Bad enough. You got a doctor with you?'

'Hell, no, this is a manhunting patrol. A known outlaw was spotted in this neck of the woods. He's wanted in connection with a bank robbery in Kettle Creek a week ago, couple of people got shot.'

'He must be mighty desperate if he headed out this way. He'd've done better making for Utah from Kettle Creek.'

Garnett scratched at his moustache, for the first time looking just a tad uneasy. 'Well, word was this country was this feller's stamping ground years ago. So I played a hunch he just might make for one of his old hideouts. We found two.' He shook his head briefly. 'Nothing, but aren't sure where there're any more . . . or even *if* there're any more.'

Logan nodded. 'You'll be out for a spell yet then.'

'No — ' Garnett said the word with a

long sigh. 'Been out too long as it is. When we saw your dust, I told my men we'd check it out and if it wasn't Chance Foran and his pard, then we'd head back for Fort Harmon.'

Logan was hard-pressed to keep a straight face when Foran's name was mentioned. 'Foran . . . ?'

The lieutenant's mouth twisted in bitterness. 'They actually had him locked-up down in Lago, but he was busted out of the local hoosegow by his pard, Durango Brown. We think they were after a getaway stake when they hit the bank at Kettle Creek.'

Logan said suddenly, 'Can you take my pard back to the fort and get him some medical treatment . . . ? He won't make it as far as Kettle Creek without proper attention.'

'I can do that.' The lieutenant was looking warily at Logan. 'You still headed for Kettle Creek, then?'

'Got a deal on the boil there — me and Coop. There was jobs going for supplying meat to the men working the new telegraph line — ' *He hoped the information was still valid: Willis had picked it up a week ago, when some pilgrim family they had eaten with one night mentioned it in casual conversation around the camp-fire. They'd agreed then that this would be their cover story if they had to explain their presence in this wild country.*

'You're likely too late. Line's gone through Kettle Creek and pushed on towards the Kaibab Plateau by now. Fact, it was the telegraph payroll Foran and Brown tried to steal . . . You get a move on you might still pick up something, but I wouldn't bet on it.'

That was good enough for Logan and he decided not to push it further. Willis was still only half-conscious and muttered a lot when the officer gave orders for a *travois* to be built but never became lucid enough to really protest.

'Obliged, Lieutenant. Tell Coop I'll get back to see him soon's I can.'

Garnett seemed a little relieved that Logan was intending to stay around the general area. He had Logan's canteens topped-up, gave him tobacco and a grub sack. After more warnings about not risking a confrontation with Chance Foran, he took his troop and rode back the way he had come, Willis dragging behind in the *travois*, lifting a hand weakly in a farewell wave.

Watching them go, Logan hoped Willis would be all right as he smoked the first decent cigarette he'd had in weeks. When the troop had dropped into a big shallow basin, out of sight, he slowly hipped in the saddle and looked towards the deep, dark bulk of Black Mesa.

Chance Foran had had an old hideout in that hole-in-the-wall at the back of the mesa. On the run as he was, it was just the kind of place Chance would make for.

Logan hoped so, anyway.

But he decided to wait until later in the afternoon before heading for the mesa, so that he would arrive when it was almost dark. He would swing wide and come in from the south or east so he wouldn't be silhouetted against the sundown skyfire.

Logan smiled faintly as he dismounted in the shade and loosened the grulla's cinchstrap: it would be good to drop in on old friends again.

Maybe.

*   *   *

His hunch paid off.

He was mildly surprised to find that Foran and Brown were actually there in the old mesa hideout they had used on and off over the years. It hadn't changed any.

It was dark in the shadow of the mesa, the western-facing side still a dull rose-gold from the sun's last fading rays. He could still recall the layout of the winding, narrow entrance with its dead-ends almost exactly. He felt a child-like elation about this, pressed against the wall low down, looking up to find direction. In minutes he was through the last tight dogleg — and smelled woodsmoke.

There was a shell already in the breech of the rifle and he kept his thumb on the hammer spur as he eased around and along the sandstone wall to his right. There was a dip at the base, behind a kind of upheaval of shale that ran for a few yards before breaking off into rubble. Foran used to plant a man up above on a ledge as lookout.

There was the fire, outside the arch of the cave he expected to find. He straightened, easing out towards the rise of the shale bar, looking for the men. One squatted at the fire. Two bedrolls were against the wall, open, likely where they had been airing in the sun during the day. But where was the second man?

He found out as, just above his head, a gun hammer snapped to full cock and Durango Brown said, 'Stop right where you are, mister!'

Logan did just that, heart hammering. He turned his head slightly and could just make out the man at the base of the ledge that led to the lookout's position. *Damn! He ought to have figured Foran wouldn't take any chances!*

'Easy on that trigger, Durango. A shot'll bring the damn cavalry troop they got looking for you.'

Silence from above, no doubt Brown surprised by Logan's voice. Then, 'Logan? That you?'

'Like Chance often says, 'as ever was, boyo'.'

'The hell you doin' here?'

'On the dodge like you two. Bluffed my way past the cavalry and played a hunch you'd be holed-up here.'

Again a short silence. 'I — I dunno about this. You just stay put! I din' like the way you was sneakin' up.'

'Hell, I didn't *know* who it was till you spoke!'

'Mmm. You always was a tricky bastard. Cavalry somewhere's out there, still, eh?'

'Somewheres. Might've moved on

but that lieutenant seemed kinda hardnosed to me. He won't give up easy.'

Durango swore and made Logan step up on the shale rock bar, as he climbed down from the ledge. Logan could maybe have shot him but didn't want to spook Foran just yet.

'Come on up and we might give you some supper — or a bullet. Depends on Chance.'

By now they were approaching the fire and Foran must have heard their voices for he was on his feet, holding a rifle at the ready when they stepped into the firelight.

He was more surprised to see Logan than Durango had been.

'You get around for a dead man,' Foran said, eyes suspicious.

'Better than lying six-feet under, staring up at daisy roots — I've got some decent grub back with my horse, Chance.' Logan grinned. 'Convinced that lieutenant I was just a poor drifter with the seat outta my pants — I'll go fetch it and bring my mount in, OK?'

'Not OK,' Foran said and started to lift his rifle again.

Durango was slightly behind Logan and off to one side and Foran's move took him by surprise. The outlaw fumbled at his rifle and, as he was closest, Logan dived for him, knocking him off his feet. Durango's rifle exploded just as Foran fired and a bullet scattered the camp-fire. Brown brought his rifle butt around and across Logan's head, knocking the man sprawling.

Head ringing, Logan kept rolling as both outlaws opened up. Lead spat gravel into his face as he wormed behind one of the saddles lying on the ground. Another bullet drove into the leather. He felt the jar, brought his rifle over and down and put two shots across the saddle. Durango Brown grunted and staggered. Foran kicked the wounded man towards Logan and lunged sideways, shooting from the hip.

Logan spun on his belly, firing into

Durango as the man made one last try to shoot him, barely a yard away. Brown lurched with the strike of the lead and was unlucky enough to fall into the path of Foran's next shot. His body spun and twisted awkwardly as he fell.

Chance Foran froze momentarily, realizing he had killed his pard and then he straightened, levering swiftly, startled as Logan came hurtling at him. Logan brought the rifle butt down across the back of Foran's head and the outlaw fell on his face and lay still.

Breathing hard, Logan felt the man's neck for a pulse, then sat back on his hams. Foran was still alive — just the way he wanted him.

'You always did have a hard head, Chance,' he said. He took a coiled rope from the saddle and began to tie the man up. 'Now you're gonna get your chance — *Chance!* — to see what the inside of a real prison looks like.'

13

Justice

Maybe because Logan's beard was dark and thick and he had long since grown back his hair, the guard on the gate of Big Mountain Penitentiary didn't recognize him.

But he knew Chance Foran, bound and gagged in the saddle, from all the wanted dodgers out on the man.

'What the hell's he doin' here?' the guard asked, an older man whose job was mainly guard duty on the gates or walls. 'You can't collect no bounty here, mister.'

Logan met his stare candidly. 'He's starting his sentence. Judge gave him ten years' hard, no parole.'

The guard blinked. 'You're kiddin'! I never heard nothin' about that! Din' even know he'd been caught!'

'Why the hell should you? You're only a guard. I gotta take Foran up to Warden Hadley.'

The man scratched at his grey hair showing beneath his hat. 'Hell, you don't just walk in here and expect to see the warden like that!'

'Listen, friend, I got orders from Judge Linus Calthorpe — *sealed* orders for Warden Hadley's eyes only — I gotta deliver this scum to no one else. Now I've had me one helluva time gettin' here and I don't aim to stay any longer than I have to, so you point me in the direction of Hadley's office, for Chris'sake, and be quick about it!'

The guard was used to being ordered about and Logan had authority in his voice and he sure looked as if he had travelled a long, hard trail. Foran was groaning into his gag and writhing in the saddle. The guard sneered.

'What's wrong with you? Don't you like it here?' He laughed briefly. 'Guarantee you *won't*! Yeah, be kinda nice to have you in our community,

Foran! You've dodged jail for a long time but seems your luck's finally run out.'

Foran wrenched wildly at his bonds and Logan glared at the gate guard. 'Will you move! The sheriff's gonna chew my ass I don't get back soon!'

The inference being that he was a deputy, just doing his job . . .

The guard 'moved', and five minutes later, Logan was escorting Foran, still with bound wrists and wearing the gag, across the edge of the work compound towards the administration buildings. Prisoners stopped to stare and maybe one or two thought he was a familiar figure but the guards soon beat them back to their jobs and another guard, younger and new since Logan had last been here, led him up the stairs to the landing at the top. The man pointed down a short corridor.

'Warden's office right there. You gonna collect the reward on this feller?'

'Who knows,' Logan growled and

shoved Foran along towards the office door.

He didn't knock, just turned the handle and stepped into Hadley's outer office.

The clerk who was always there at his small desk, copying reports and handling the paperwork of the prison as Hadley passed it out to him, snapped his head up irritably. He was in his forties and had worked for Hadley for the four years the man had been stationed here as warden. He stared at Foran and then at Logan, but his eyes showed no recognition.

'What do you want? This is Warden Hadley's office — '

'I want to see him. Gotta deliver this prisoner in person and don't gimme any more delays! The warden's waitin' to get his hands on this Chance Foran and if I have to tell him I been given the run-around by his guards and now you, he won't be happy.'

The clerk was already moving around the desk and hurrying towards the inner door. He swallowed as he knocked on the rippled glass panel and opened the door. Logan stiffened slightly as he heard the hated voice bark,

'Did you hear me give you permission to enter, Harris?'

'Sir! There — there's a man here, a deputy or a bounty hunter or something, and he has — he has Chuck Foran prisoner and says he must deliver him to you — right away!'

A brief stunned silence ensued, during which time Logan thrust the staggering Foran into Hadley's office and, using the outlaw as a part shield, said in a deep, disguised voice, 'With Judge Calthorpe's compliments, Warden. He's yours for the next ten years. If you let him live that long.'

Those last words froze whatever words Hadley was about to utter. He frowned and stared at the dishevelled figure standing across his desk with an outlaw bound and gagged, held steady by his left hand. Hadley was impeccably

233

dressed as usual. Then beads of sweat suddenly started out of his forehead as he waved his clerk out. The door closed with a dull click and Hadley cleared his throat.

'This — is — out of order! For one thing, I do not know any Judge Calthorpe and I have received no notification from *anyone* that I was to expect this. *Who* did my clerk say it was . . . Chance Foran?'

'You heard right, Warden,' Logan said in his natural voice, watching closely, seeing the puzzled shadow behind Hadley's eyes as memories began to stir. But Logan barely resembled the rake-thin, shaven-headed prisoner who had last stood there, months ago, in a sagging, filthy uniform.

But suspicions had been aroused and Logan smiled thinly. 'He might be willing to tell you where he stashed that loot from the Dogwood bank, Warden. You'll have him all to yourself now and you can whip him or torture him as much as you like until he gives you the info you want.'

Hadley sat down slowly and eased around in his chair, mopping his face. Then he stared with distaste at the sodden kerchief, started to open a drawer as if to get a fresh one or dispose of the one he held.

Logan's six gun came out of leather and Hadley froze. 'Leave it, Hadley. Here's the real deal: I'll give you this scum in exchange for Laurie Carson.'

Hadley stiffened, his face pale as a floursack.

His mouth worked and the words came out raggedly.

'Who — ? Wha — ?' He paused, breath audible as he cleared his throat noisily. His eyes suddenly widened. 'No! My God, it can't be!' He stood as if a spring had shot him out of his chair and Logan cocked his gun hammer threateningly. Warden Lester Hadley shook his head several times, unbelievingly. 'You — you can't be Logan Breck!'

Logan smiled through his dusty

beard. 'Been a long time since I've had my own head of hair, Warden, but it's me and this is really Chance Foran. Get Crow Delaney up here, with Boyd Lee and tell them to bring Laurie Carson with them.' His voice hardened and sudden fear flared in Hadley's face but then the old Hadley began to show again, the one in control of *his* penitentiary.

'Oh, dear me, you have made a blunder, haven't you, Breck! Such a serious one, too. Yes, I thought Crow's idea of holding the girl hostage in order to bring you out of hiding was quite excellent, considering the man's usual display of half-witted intelligence. I believed it would take some time for you to come, but — *here you are!* Of your own volition, trying to ram a 'deal' down my throat, *in my own office!*' He shook his head vigorously. 'Oh, no! We can't have that, and we most certainly do not do business that way! *I* call the shots, Breck! Didn't you learn anything while you were here?'

'I learnt what a corrupt, hypocritcal son of a bitch you are, and . . . '

Logan saw something move out of the corner of his left eye, slightly to one side of Hadley's desk. The curtains parted and Crow Delaney stood there with a sawn-off shotgun held in both hands. Boyd Lee was holding the cord that drew the drapes aside from the small door hidden in the wall behind. Delaney jerked the shotgun.

'Put the gun away, Logan. No, better still, lower the hammer and put it on the desk!' The shotgun's yawning barrels emphasized Delaney's words and Logan hesitated only briefly before obeying. Delaney glanced enquiringly at Hadley who nodded curtly, his face hardening in bleak lines now he knew he was safe once more. 'OK, untie Foran.'

Logan obeyed and stepped back as Foran made the expected swing at his face. But the man's arms were still numbed and heavy from the bonds and he missed, stood there, glaring, rubbing each arm alternately, wincing as blood began to circulate again.

Hadley lit a cigar, at ease behind his desk now, looking almost amused. 'You surely are a handful, Logan! Too bad we couldn't have hit it off better. However, no matter now. You have just set my record straight: *No escapes from Big Mountain during my tenure!* A perfect record — I suppose I should thank you in some way.' He pretended to think about it and then said to Boyd Lee, 'Bring up the girl. We'll allow him to see her for a few minutes before we . . . settle things.'

Logan was poised like a panther on a ledge above a browsing goat, ready to spring and subdue its target. By now Foran's hands had feeling again, enough for him to hit Logan in the kidneys, and, when the man fell to his knees, to kick him in the side and stretch him out on the floor. Nostrils white, he stepped in to deliver more violence but at a lifted finger from Hadley, Crow hit Foran with the shotgun, hard, across the side of the head.

The outlaw grunted and fell to his knees, bent forward, holding his bleeding head and moaning softly.

He was sitting against the wall when Boyd returned with the girl. Leering, he thrust her into the room. Logan moved towards her, fighting down a surge of murderous rage that knifed through him. Crow made to step in but Logan straight-armed him out of the way and such was the deadly look on his face that Delaney took it. Boyd Lee decided not to make any move. Hadley didn't appear concerned and watched with that cold, detached half-smile as Logan folded his arms about the frail, ill-treated girl.

Despite her ordeal and her condition, Laurie did not burst into tears but clung to him with desperate strength in her thin arms, pressed her bruised and swollen face into his chest. He held her firmly, one hand moving gently up and down her back, feeling the notches of her spine. *By God someone would pay dearly for her mistreatment!*

'I'm here now, Laurie,' was all he said and after a minute, she lifted her face to look up into his.

'I've prayed hard enough for this moment,' she whispered.

'Savour it, my dear,' Hadley said abruptly. 'It may well be the only consolation you will have.' He beamed around the room. 'This is nothing short of marvellous! All gathered here where I am in complete control and can end it to my satisfaction with just a snap of my fingers!'

Logan set his chiselled gaze on the Warden and Hadley briefly showed a little apprehension. 'You don't need Laurie now. You have me, and you have Foran. I can be returned to the prison population . . . '

'Dad, no!' Laurie was horrified but he continued in that icy tone: ' . . . and Foran can be made to talk and tell you where he's hid that bank money. Do the decent thing and let the girl go, see she gets safely to Papago Wells.'

Hadley laughed. 'You don't honestly believe I would agree to that, surely, Logan!'

Breck sighed and shook his head slowly. 'No, I guess not.'

'Perhaps you have an alternative request?'

'No other request — but there is an alternative: if you don't agree, you'll die.'

Hadley's expression didn't change. 'Ah!' He spread his arms. 'And how shall you achieve this?'

'You agree or not?'

Hadley's face clouded. 'Stop this nonsense! I've had enough! You are both at my mercy — though I believe I may have misplaced that right now!' He paused and glanced at Crow and Boyd, waiting for the expected appreciation of his small joke — and got it when the men realized what he was doing. They grinned, nudged each other. Hadley, satisfied, looked smug and pointed a finger at Logan, 'I have no further use for you.' He flicked the finger then at the girl. 'You, too, have become superfluous, my dear, so I will leave your ultimate fate to Mr Delaney and Mr Lee . . . '

Logan started forward but the shotgun's barrels rammed into his side and he sagged against the wall, gasping, holding his lower ribs.

Foran, now leaning against the wall, growled, 'What about me?' His voice was harsh and showed desperation.

Hadley pursed his lips. 'Yes, what about you, Foran? I would really like to get my hands on some of that money you stole from the Dogwood bank, but so much time has gone by — and I believe you and your partner, Durango Brown, attempted a hold-up of the Kettle Creek bank. Somehow, I don't believe you would have tried to rob that bank if you still had access to the money from Dogwood. So, your usefulness to me is, at best, debatable.'

Foran smiled crookedly. 'Not from where I stand. We needed money to get back to where we stashed the Dogwood cash. That's why we hit Kettle Creek. It ought to be safe to spend that dinero now — hundred-dollar bills are gettin' as common as assholes these days.'

Hadley seemed thoughtful. 'We-ell, perhaps — and perhaps you believe you can fool me into keeping you alive a little longer? Yes, all right. You can live — for now. But I warn you, you will be interrogated by Mr Delaney here and he was trained in his somewhat crude but effective methods by the one and only Collie — I'm sure you've heard some of the rumours about him that have reached beyond these walls.'

Foran looked anxious. 'Listen, I wasn't bein' smart-ass! I do have that money stashed away! I can take you to it.'

Hadley's laugh cut off Foran's words abruptly.

'I think you may have hit him just a little too hard, Crow! You hear what he said: he can take me to the money! Dear me, he must think we are a bunch of hill-billies here . . . '

Suddenly, Hadley's eyes almost started from their sockets. Everyone had been giving their attention to Foran and Hadley and during that time, Logan had sagged lower, still gasping for breath, no one taking any particular notice of him. Then Laurie had gone to his side to help him.

Abruptly, he straightened, thrust her roughly aside. She gave a small cry of alarm and fell at one end of the desk. At the same time, Logan's right hand came up grasping Cooper Willis's derringer boot gun. The top barrel flashed and Crow Delaney staggered back, a ball through the bridge of his nose. The shotgun began to fall and Boyd made a lunge for it as Hadley frantically reached into his desk drawer and pulled out a small handgun.

Logan swung the derringer onto Boyd, last of the men who had raped his daughter, and fired coldly. The ball took Boyd in the neck. He shrieked as he went down on one knee, bright blood gushing over his collar, dropping the shotgun. Laurie reached for it but Foran knocked her aside, dived across and snatched it up as Hadley fired in panic. His bullet grazed Foran's shoulder and he sat back against the wall with a jolt, the Greener in his lap. One barrel thundered and Hadley was blown into the heavy curtain, dragging it off the rail, holding rings popping one by one as he clawed at the fabric with a death grip, his chest blasted open in one gaping raw wound.

Logan snatched his own six gun from the edge of the desk and spun towards Foran as the outlaw bared his teeth and brought up the smoking shotgun. Laurie screamed and Logan threw himself in a headlong dive, shooting in mid-air as the second barrel blasted. Buckshot punched a hole in the door and when the smoke cleared, Logan, now on the floor on his side, Colt cocked and ready for another shot, saw Foran sprawled in a heap, two fresh bullet holes in his chest.

He had taken one chance too many. And lost.

* * *

The prison was now back into some semblance of order. Soldiers with rifles and fixed bayonets, herded the gossiping, curious prisoners into the work compound. Those still out with the road gangs would be brought in later under guard: half a dozen had already made a break and were being hunted.

Lieutenant Joshua Garnett wiped sweat from his face and half-smiled at Logan as he sat over drinks at a table under the *galeria* that had once been favoured by Hadley for his evening meals, facing west into the blazing sunset.

Laurie, looking somewhat better and cleaner in fresh feminine clothes thoughtfully brought by Garnett, pushed a strand of hair away from her pinched face. She would be some weeks recovering fully and putting back some of the weight she had lost during her ordeal. But her father would see she regained her good health again, no matter how long it took.

She reached a hand across the table and touched his arm. He smiled at her, took her hand in his, looking at Garnett. 'Coop's definitely going to be all right now?'

'Yes, tough as petrified wood. He actually wanted to ride with us after he came round enough to tell me what you had in mind, tracking down Foran and so on. The doctor says, thanks to that thread you had draining the wound he should make a full recovery in a couple of weeks. Good work, Mr Carson.'

Garnett steadied his gaze on Logan's face but got no response. Laurie said, 'I'm proud to call him 'uncle', Lieutenant. I owe him my life.'

'Of course, ma'am — I suppose it's only what you should expect from a loving — uncle, eh?' He settled his campaign hat squarely on his head, standing now. 'There'll be some sort of enquiry, because Hadley was a chief warden, but from my preliminary investigation it seems obvious he was just unlucky enough to be caught in the crossfire. That's what my report will say, anyway.' He gave them both a brief salute. 'I wish you both good luck.'

'Thanks, Lieutenant,' Logan said feeling the relief wash through him like a wave, leaving him feeling relaxed, for the first time in many a moon.

'I don't think I can go back to school, Dad,' Laurie said quietly. 'After all it is a school for 'young ladies' and I — I'm hardly that now, am I?'

He turned to her quickly, saw the tears brimming. He squeezed her hand. 'You'll always be a lady to me, Laurie. You don't need any special school for that.'

She smiled, fighting the tears. 'That's all that matters, really, what you think of me. That old Indian, U-Sha, told me that. He said he would be in your debt as long as he lived . . . When he heard there was a white girl searching for him, and that I was your daughter, he sent men out to look for me. It was lucky they found me just after the snake bit me, took me to the *pueblo* where they nursed me — until . . . '

Her voice choked off. He knew she was thinking of Delaney's murderous raid. Now the tears welled despite her struggle to hold them back.

'They killed them all, Dad — mercilessly! All because Hadley wanted me as a — a hostage!'

He slid his arm about her shoulders, holding her firmly. 'You can't take any of the blame, Laurie. They did the murdering. You were just as much one of the victims as any of old U-Sha's Navajos.' He tilted her chin and looked down directly into the moist eyes. 'That's all behind you now, Laurie — leave it there. Got any plans?'

She made an effort at control, worked up a small smile. 'There's still money enough left to buy us a small ranch.'

He grinned. 'Sounds good. But we'll

look for some prove-up land so you can keep your money for that accountancy thing you want to try. Coop can help me build up the spread while you get your staff and so on set up. Anyway, I might even get a reward for capturing Foran. Then we'll be sitting pretty.'

Her eyes glinted mischievously. 'I might've known you'd be stubborn about it and have some other plan all worked out! But I like the idea — just as long as we're together and can find a little peace and quiet.'

'Amen to that, but it'll take some getting used to!'

'We'll have plenty of time, Dad, plenty of time.'

Her smile was warm and confident and he reached for his glass on the table, and raised it as the rays of the setting sun touched it, making it flash like crystal.

'I'll drink to that,' he said.

We do hope that you have enjoyed reading this large print book.

Did you know that all of our titles are available for purchase?

We publish a wide range of high quality large print books including:
Romances, Mysteries, Classics General Fiction Non Fiction and Westerns

Special interest titles available in large print are:
The Little Oxford Dictionary Music Book, Song Book Hymn Book, Service Book

Also available from us courtesy of Oxford University Press:
Young Readers' Dictionary (large print edition) Young Readers' Thesaurus (large print edition)

For further information or a free brochure, please contact us at:
Ulverscroft Large Print Books Ltd., The Green, Bradgate Road, Anstey, Leicester, LE7 7FU, England. Tel: (00 44) **0116 236 4325 Fax:** (00 44) **0116 234 0205**

TRAVIS

Richard Wyler

Jim Travis had every penny of his hard-earned savings in Sweetwater's bank. It was his future — but when Luke Parsons and his wild bunch cleaned out the town's bank, Jim's money was part of the haul. With no help from the town, Jim rode out to retrieve his money, trailing the Parsons bunch across wild territory. Parsons threw everything he had at the lone rider dogging his heels, yet Jim kept on coming — and forced a final, savage showdown.

A ROPE FOR SCUDDER

Clay More

Jake Scudder hauled Hank Lassiter from the jaws of death three times in twenty-four hours. Yet within a couple of days he had been found guilty of murder, sentenced to death and set en route to the penitentiary to be hanged. However, Scudder was given a chance for redemption — but it meant he would have to rescue the victim's niece, and discover who had set him up. Whoever it was had much to answer for . . .

GUNSMOKE MOUNTAIN

Owen G. Irons

When Wyoming rancher Amos Corbett's daughter is abducted, Dan Featherskill is offered the job of finding her. A skilled mountain man, Dan turns down the job when Corbett demands that he also kill Celia's abductor. Two hardcases are set upon the trail, but when they threaten the ranch of Deucie Campbell, the mountain girl who once loved Dan, he has to take a hand. And then a winter storm grips Shadow Mountain and all hell breaks loose across the timberland.

THE STAGE TO COOPER'S CREEK

Tom Benson

Carrying two passengers and money for the local bank, the stage to Cooper's Creek left Tombstone and never arrived — it just vanished. Cooper's Creek becomes the scene of shootouts, and Marshal Willard, accompanied by a young investigator, is soon headed for a deserted mining town. They find what they are looking for, except for one missing parcel. Only an old miner can tell them what happened — but can they track him down and get him to talk?